Mia's
sweet
surprises

SIMON SPOTLIGHT

An imprint of Simon & Schuster Children's Publishing Division
1230 Avenue of the Americas, New York, New York 10020
First Simon Spotlight paperback edition May 2021
Copyright © 2021 by Simon & Schuster, Inc.
All rights reserved, including the right of reproduction
in whole or in part in any form.
SIMON SPOTLIGHT and colophon are registered trademarks of
Simon & Schuster, Inc.
Text by Tracey West
Chapter header illustrations by Laura Roode
Designed by Laura Roode
For information about special discounts for bulk purchases, please contact
Simon & Schuster Special Sales at 1-866-506-1949
or business@simonandschuster.com.
Manufactured in the United States of America 0321 OFF
2 4 6 8 10 9 7 6 5 3 1
ISBN 978-1-5344-8544-0 (hc)
ISBN 978-1-5344-8543-3 (pbk)
ISBN 978-1-5344-8545-7 (eBook)
Library of Congress Control Number 2021933876

CUPCAKE DIARIES

Mia's sweet surprises

by coco simon

Simon Spotlight

New York   London   Toronto   Sydney   New Delhi

CHAPTER 1

Black Is My New Favorite Color

I lay on a beach chair in my backyard under the big maple tree, staring up at the undersides of the tree leaves. It was a hot Friday afternoon in July, and I'd been in the chair for an hour, listening to the bees buzz and the birds chirp, and not doing much else.

Then I heard my mom's voice drift through the kitchen window.

"I just don't know what happened, Sharon," Mom was saying as she talked to the mom of my best friend Katie. "One minute she was my sweet and smiley Mia, and the next she's wearing black and moping around."

I looked down at the short black sleeveless dress I was wearing. I'd made it myself. I love to design clothes, and I watch fashion show competitions on TV, and recently, I saw a designer who made this all-black collection and fell in love. She wore only black herself, and I thought she looked seriously cool and put together. I'd decided to go mono-chromatic and see how I liked it. But because I'd chosen to do this during the summer, Mom—along with my stepdad, Eddie, and my stepbrother, Dan, thought it was weird.

My mom laughed. "Yes, I suppose there are worse things than going through a goth phase," she said.

I sighed. Mom was getting it all wrong. I had no urge to listen to sad music. I just thought black was classy and looked cool!

"Mmm-hmm," Mom continued. "Yes, I think she probably does miss Katie. But she understands that this is a busy time in Katie's life right now."

Mom had finally said something right. I *did* miss Katie, which was silly since it had been only nine-teen days (yes, I was counting) since I'd last seen her. That was on the day her mom had gotten mar-ried, and the Cupcake Club had baked ten dozen cupcakes for the reception, and I had made a Katie a beautiful pink bridesmaid's dress to wear. We had so much fun!

And then the next morning, Katie had gone to spend a week with her grandparents while her mom and Mr. Green (Katie's stepdad, and also a math teacher at our school) went on a honeymoon. And after Katie returned she'd been too busy setting up her new house to hang out.

That's why, after the wedding, my summer had just sort of fizzled out. The Cupcake Club had no upcoming orders; except for our standing order with Mona at The Special Day wedding boutique. Thank goodness people were still getting married, and girls still wanted to be beautiful brides. Alexis had gone on vacation with her family, and Emma was busy with modeling jobs now that school was out.

My vacation with Mom, Eddie, and Dan wasn't scheduled until the end of August. And in a few days, I was supposed to spend some time with my dad in the city. We'd probably do the usual things— museums, go out to eat, see a Broadway show. Dad always made sure we did something fun every day.

But the past few weeks—they'd been a big stretch of nothing. And without Katie it was almost unbearable.

I'd started out binge-watching fashion competition shows. Then I'd gotten inspired to create my all-black wardrobe, and I'd started sewing and shopping with my Cupcake earnings. But I'd also been sleeping until noon every day, and chilling out under this maple tree and staring at stuff. And I guess that's what had Mom worried.

Mom was still talking to Katie's mom. "Yes, I think the baking session later will do them all good. . . . You don't mind? Great, thanks, Sharon!"

Then Mom yelled out the window at me.

"Mia, Katie's mom is going to be here at four to take you to Emma's!" she said. "Just make sure you're ready by then. And awake!"

"Ha-ha!" I yelled back. Why did it matter how late I slept, or how much? It's not like I had anything better to do. Why do parents have to make such a big deal about *everything*?

I looked at my phone. It was two o'clock. Two hours to go. I got up from the chair, stretched, and then headed up to my room to change.

I take fashion design classes, so my bedroom looks more like a sewing studio. I've got a special table for my sewing machine, and there is a stack of plastic bins to hold my fabric, thread, scissors, and other supplies. A few months ago I saved up and got a dress form—that's the thing that looks like a mannequin, but it has no head, arms, or legs—in my size. You use it to make patterns when you're designing clothes so you can see how something will look and fit. It's very cool, but it takes up a lot of room.

I knew a sleeveless dress wouldn't be the best outfit for baking cupcakes, so I slipped on a black tunic and black capris leggings with black flats. As I looked in the mirror, I thought about how much white flour and white powdered sugar flies everywhere when we bake, and realized that might be a problem.

"I guess I could wear an apron," I said out loud, but the only one I had was a white one with pink cupcakes on it that my aunt had given me for Christmas. It was cute, but it would definitely spoil my whole look.

I glanced at the yards of black fabric messily draped over my chair. A black apron couldn't be too hard, could it? I looked online and found directions for a simple bib apron. I cleared off my sewing table and sketched out the pattern on some white pattern paper—its lightweight and comes in big sheets. I cut out the pattern and then found some black cotton fabric that felt like it would be good for an apron.

Then I ironed the fabric, pinned the pattern to

it, cut out the pieces, pinned the hems, and started sewing. It may sound like a lot of steps, but an apron is a pretty simple thing to sew, so it didn't take long. I even added a big pocket in the front. I was finishing up when I heard Mom yell upstairs, "Mia, Katie and her mom are waiting for you!"

"Coming!" I yelled back, and rolled up my apron and stuck that into a bag with my phone. Then I ran down the stairs and past my mom.

"What? No good-bye hug?" she asked.

I stopped in my tracks and hugged her.

"Have fun," Mom said. I ran out to join Katie in the backseat of her mom's car. She was wearing a shirt from one her 5K runs and a pair of denim shorts.

"MIA!" Katie crushed me with a hug, and suddenly, it felt like no time had passed since I'd seen her. "I missed you."

"I missed you, too," I said. I squinted at her face. "You've got freckles on your face!"

"Grandma Carole took me to the beach a lot," she explained. "I always wear sunscreen, but it didn't stop the freckles, I guess."

"They're so cute!" I told her.

Katie's mom looked into the rearview mirror. "Mia, I just want to thank you again for all your help with the wedding. The pictures came back, and the dresses look wonderful."

Like I said, I had made Katie a dress for the wedding and helped her mom redesign an old dress she had so she could wear it as a wedding gown.

"Thanks, Mrs. B—are you still Mrs. Brown? Or are you Mrs. Green?" I asked.

"Well, I thought a lot about it," she answered. "I'm going to stay Mrs. Brown so that Katie and I will have the same last name. I almost went with Brown-Green, but that sounds like I'm a crayon or something."

I laughed. "It does!"

Katie and I talked about her visit with her grandmother and the work on the new house, and she caught me up by the time we reached Emma's house.

When we got out of the car, the smell of a cookout reached my nose. A bunch of boys, including Emma's brother Matt, were playing basketball in the driveway and blaring loud music. I looked at Katie.

"This should be a fun baking session," I said.

The front door was cracked open, so we walked inside the house and found Emma in the kitchen with Alexis, setting up the baking ingredients.

"Katie!" they both squealed, and rushed over to her. They hadn't seen me in weeks, either, but I understand the excitement about Katie. Her whole life had changed so much, and it was nice to see that her life with us hadn't changed.

"It's really good to see everybody," Katie said. "Plus, I'm happy to be baking again. We're still organizing the kitchen at the new house, so I haven't baked there yet."

"Well, you know, it's just vanilla mini cupcakes, nothing exciting," Emma said, pushing a strand of blond hair behind her ear. "Mona increased her order, so we need to make more than usual. She says the bridal business is booming."

"Your mom started a trend, Katie," I joked.

"Mom's going to help me bring these to her bridal shop tomorrow because I'm modeling some bridesmaid's dresses for Mona, anyway," Emma continued. "We just have to bake and pack tonight. Dad's grilling outside so we've got the kitchen to ourselves."

"Great! Let's get baking!" Katie said eagerly.

"And we also need to discuss new orders," Alexis reminded us. She was the only one of us wearing an official pink Cupcake Club T-shirt. "They're starting to pick up, and we've got to figure out our plan for the summer festival. That's just a few weeks away."

"Finally, something fun to do in this town," I said.

"Really, Mia?" Alexis asked. "I mean, I know we're not New York City, but there's plenty to do in Maple Grove. You've never complained before."

I sighed. "I guess I've just been kind of bored, with all of you being so busy."

"Oh, you missed us!" Katie cried. "No worries, Mia. I don't have anything else exciting planned for the summer. And aren't you going to be away, like, for most of August? Then it'll be our turn to be lonely without you."

I tied on my black apron, and Katie started measuring out flour. Alexis began to put liners in the mini cupcake pans, while Emma brought eggs out of the fridge. She set them down on the counter, and we chatted a little bit while we waited for the eggs to lose their chill. (Room temperature eggs are better for baking.) We had baked these cupcakes so many times that we had a rhythm down.

"A week in a cabin with Mom, Eddie, and Dan, and a million mosquitos is not exactly worth getting excited about," I said as I measured out the sugar for the batter. "I'm lucky Mom's letting me leave early for a week at fashion design camp."

"My mom says you started wearing only black." Katie looked me up and down. "You look nice, but you look really different from normal Mia."

"'Normal Mia'? I'm not even sure what that means," I said.

"Well, I think it's pretty smart," Alexis said. "Look at Steve Jobs—you know, that guy who ran Apple? He wore the same black turtleneck, jeans, and sneakers every day. It let him concentrate on his business and not have to worry about what he was wearing."

Emma's eyes widened. "The same? You mean he never washed them?"

"That would be gross!" Katie cried.

Alexis laughed. "No, I mean like he bought a lot of the exact same thing so he could wear the same outfit every day."

"I get it, but that's not why I'm doing it," I said. "I . . . I just like wearing black, that's all."

"Mona has a whole line of black bridesmaid's dresses," Emma said. "They're very popular for nighttime weddings."

Then Katie turned on the mixer, and we stopped talking because the mixer gets really loud. We worked quickly, getting the batter into pans to make seven dozen cupcakes—six dozen for the order, plus some extra for tasting, to make sure we're delivering a good product. And also because whenever we bake cupcakes, everyone close by descends on us and asks for one.

That's what happened as soon as we put the cupcakes on racks to cool. Matt and his three friends came into the kitchen.

"Hi, Matt," Alexis said, smiling.

"Hi, Alexis," Matt said, and Katie looked at me and waggled her eyebrows. Alexis and Matt were always flirting.

"Matt, you guys need to get out of here," Emma said. "Mom said we could have the kitchen."

"We're thirsty," Matt replied, and opened the refrigerator and took out a pitcher of water. His friends began to hover around the cupcakes.

"Emma, can we have some?" Matt asked.

Emma rolled her eyes. "Dad's going to have dinner ready soon. Can't you wait? They're not even frosted."

Alexis walked over to Matt. I saw her put a hand on Matt's arm and then whisper, "It's okay. We always make extra." Matt grinned at her.

Emma grabbed Alexis by the elbow. "Come on—let's go talk about that summer festival."

We followed Emma out to her backyard and sat at the picnic table.

"I hope you girls are hungry!" her dad called out to us. "I'm making enough burgers to feed an army! I've got plenty of veggie burgers, too."

"Mmmmmm," Katie said.

"Business, then burgers," Alexis said.

"The Maple Grove Summer Street Festival is in two weeks?" I asked.

Alexis nodded. "We've paid the fifty-dollar vendor fee. If we want to make a profit, we'll need to sell at least eighteen cupcakes."

"No problem!" Katie said. "I bet we could sell a hundred and eighty!"

"I think we should do chocolate and vanilla," Emma said. "Keep it simple, so we can make a lot of cupcakes. And everyone likes either chocolate or vanilla."

Alexis nodded. "That makes a lot of sense."

Katie agreed. "It does, but what about our Daisy Donuts problem?"

"What do you mean?" I asked.

"That new doughnut shop in town," Katie said. "Every morning they've got a line that goes down the block. Mom and I waited on it for twenty minutes the other morning, and I saw a sign that they're going to be selling at the festival. They're serious competition."

Alexis frowned. "They'll take all our business. Unless . . . Were their doughnuts any good?"

"Delicious!" Katie said. "They've got amazing flavors. Pink lemonade, apple pie, birthday cake . . ."

"Maybe we need to do some of *our* amazing flavors, then," I said, "so we can compete."

"No problem!" Katie said. "You know we can come up with something great. We've done it before."

Just then Matt and his friends strolled into the yard.

"Those cupcakes were great, but why were they so tiny?" Matt asked. "I could have easily eaten four more."

Emma's head whipped toward him. "What do you mean 'four *more*'? How many did you eat?"

"Four each," Matt replied.

"Nooooo!" Katie wailed. "We baked only an extra dozen. But four boys and four cupcakes each is . . ."

"Sixteen!" Emma finished. "Seriously, Matt?"

"Alexis said we could," Matt said, and Emma turned to Alexis, who was bright red.

"Did you really say that?" Emma asked.

"I said we always made extra, so they could have some," Alexis said defensively. "How was I supposed to know they were going to eat four each!"

Emma threw up her hands. "Great! What do we do now?"

CHAPTER 2

A Super Blah Summer

$\mathcal{K}$atie jumped up. "Don't worry. I'll get another batch of batter started."

"I have an even better idea," Emma said. She pointed at Matt. "We're not going to make the new cupcakes. You guys are."

One of Matt's friends looked uncomfortable. "Yeah, well, I gotta go."

"Me too," said the second friend, and they both left.

One friend remained—a boy with curly black hair. "I'll help," he said. "I like to bake."

"Thanks, Miles," Emma said, and shot Matt a look to show him she was still mad at him.

"Are we seriously doing this?" Matt asked.

"Seriously," Emma said, and we went back

into the kitchen. Emma pointed to the sink.

"The first thing you need to do is wash out the mixing bowl," she said.

Matt shook his head. "I can't believe I'm doing this."

Miles looked at the ingredients still on the kitchen counter. "Do you have any softened butter for your batter, or do you use vegetable oil?"

Katie looked at him with admiration. "Butter," she said. "We don't have any softened, but we can—"

"Soften it in the microwave," Miles finished.

Katie, Miles, and Matt got to work on making a new dozen mini cupcakes, and Alexis and Emma started frosting the ones the boys hadn't eaten. I sat down at the kitchen table and took out my sketchbook.

Maple Grove Summer Street Festival, I thought. What kind of cupcakes would stand out and be a hit? I scrolled through my phone for ideas, and there were some cute ones, but nothing inspired me. Little teddy-bear–shaped crackers lying on chewing gum/towels like they were on a cupcake beach? Nah. Cupcakes with graham cracker "sand" on top and little paper umbrellas stuck into them? Cute, but they didn't do anything for me.

I closed my eyes and tried to picture the perfect

summer cupcake. A cupcake with black frosting popped into my mind, and while I thought that would be a totally cool look for a cupcake, I knew it wasn't summery.

What color is summery? I wondered. Yellow like the sun? Blue like swimming pool water?

I started absently sketching circles—perfect, round circles. Such a classic shape! I sketched a cupcake with smooth blue frosting and a perfectly round, slightly darker blue circle on the top. Simple and elegant.

"All right, we've got six dozen ready," I heard Alexis say.

"And one more going in the oven!" Katie called out.

Emma walked over to the table and looked over my shoulder. "Blue on blue?

"Like the colors of the ocean," I said. "But simple. Elegant."

Katie joined us. "It's pretty, but that seems like it would be better for a classy event, like an engagement party. I think we need something that people are going to talk about. Maybe a cute clown face made of candy?"

I shuddered. "Clowns are creepy," I said.

"Maybe," Emma agreed. "But I think Katie's

right. We need something really special. What about cute animal faces? Like turtles?"

I started to sketch. I drew two eyes, circles with black dots inside them. Then I drew a mouth and added a tongue sticking out.

"That's cute, but I'm not sure how we'd do that with candy," Katie said.

I put down my pencil. "I don't know. I'm just not feeling it."

"You're really not feeling very colorful," Emma remarked.

I shrugged. "I can create only what I'm inspired to create. And right now, the only thing inspiring me is the color black."

"Maybe we need to feed you some rainbow candy," Emma teased.

"Or unicorn tears," Katie added.

Emma frowned. "Are unicorn tears colorful?"

"Of course they are," Katie said. "Everything on a unicorn is colorful. And they're tears of happiness, not sadness."

Suddenly the voice of Emma's dad rang through the kitchen.

"Time to eat, troops!"

We went back out to the yard, where the rest of Emma's family had gathered: Emma's mom; her little brother, Jake; and her oldest brother, Sam. Everyone in the family had Emma's bright blue eyes and blond hair.

We put food on our plates, and Katie, Emma, Alexis, and I sat together.

"I think we should think of some ideas for the festival on our own and then have another meeting next weekend," Katie said. "Mom said our house will be ready, and we can do it there."

"You'll have to do it without me," I said. "Dad's picking me up on Tuesday for my week with him."

"Oh no!" Katie cried. "Is that so soon?"

"Maybe we can do something before I go," I suggested. "You could come over and hang out."

"Do I have to wear all black if I come over?" Alexis teased.

"Cut it out," I said, feeling a little annoyed. "I'm just doing what I like. You do you."

Katie nodded. "You do you too."

Then a timer beeped on her phone, and she jumped up. "Time to get the cupcakes out of the oven!" she said, and ran inside.

Then Sam starting playing some music on a wireless speaker, and Jake started running around squirting everyone with a water blaster, and dinner turned into a party. Alexis and Matt retreated

19

to two camp chairs in the corner of the yard and started talking. Katie and Miles were scrolling through their phones, looking at baking recipes. I moved to a lounge chair and stared up at the trees. *Just like at home,* I thought, suddenly feeling superblah again.

Then I saw Emma leaning over me.

"Mia, come on. Let's dance!" she said.

"I don't feel like it," I replied.

"Come on!" she urged. "Everybody's dancing."

She nodded to the left, where I saw all my friends and Emma's family were indeed up and dancing around.

"I'm just not in the mood," I said.

Emma cupped her hands around her mouth. "Jake!" she yelled.

Jake came running over, holding his water blaster, his T-shirt soaked with water.

"What?" he asked.

"Squirt Mia if she doesn't get up to dance," Emma said.

"No way!" I protested. I hate getting wet. "All right, all right, I'll dance."

Emma grabbed me by the arm, and I joined in. Luckily, Sam has good taste in music, and soon I was moving to the beat.

Katie grabbed my hands and twirled me around.

"I think this is even better than unicorn tears, right?" she asked.

I smiled. "Maybe. But I guess we'll never know."

But the more we danced, the more I found myself smiling.

CHAPTER 3

Plans with Dad

The next day I was back to feeling blah. I was still asleep at eleven a.m. when the voice of Eddie, woke me up.

"Mia, your dad's on the phone!" he yelled up the stairs. "He says he's been trying to call your cell, but you haven't been answering."

I groaned and stretched and picked up my phone. Three missed calls from Dad. Was there some kind of emergency?

"Please tell him to hang up, and I'll call him now!" I yelled back.

"You got it, sleepyhead!" Eddie replied. He loves to tease me about my sleeping habits.

I sat up and dialed Dad.

"Mia! Sorry to wake you up," he said.

"It's okay," I said, yawning. "What's up?"

"I have a proposition for you about our week coming up," he said. "I know we were planning to do the usual things, but now I'm thinking we could go on a little trip."

I sat up straighter, my mind racing. Would we fly to Paris? Or visit Puerto Rico to meet his cousins, like he sometimes talks about?

Dad cleared his throat. "My college reunion is next weekend," he began, and my hopes of a glamorous vacation sank. "I wasn't planning to go, but then I got a call from my friend Toshi. I went to college with him and his wife, Ayumi, and they ended up getting married and having some kids. Anyway, Toshi asked if I was coming to the reunion, and I told him I couldn't because it was my week with you, but he invited us to come stay with him for a few days."

"Like, in their house?" I asked. Not only was my image of staying in a fancy Paris hotel gone, but it was replaced by sleeping on a cot in some random basement.

"They're really cool," Dad said. "Their son, Kai, is a bit older than you, but their daughter, Tamiko, is your age. So you'd have someone to hang out with."

I wasn't sure what to think. Dad had never suggested a trip like this before, so on the one hand it would be fun to do something different with him. On the other hand, it could end up being a really boring week.

Then I thought about how bored I'd been the last few weeks, and it didn't seem so bad. Still, I had questions.

"How long is a few days?" I asked.

"Just three or four days with the Satos, but with traveling days on either end," Dad replied. "That will give me time to do the reunion events, and both of us time to hit the beach."

"There's a beach? You could have mentioned that first," I said.

Dad laughed. "Yes, they live in the beach town called Bayville, with cute shops and a little boardwalk," he said. "But if you don't want to go, I'll understand. And if you're uncomfortable staying with the Satos, we can book a hotel. You'd just have to say the word."

I've heard of Bayville, it's only about ten or fifteen minutes away from Maple Grove. But funnily enough, I've never been there. A short trip to a beach town sounded really adorable. And Dad sounded so happy about the idea.

"Let's do it," I said.

"Great!" Dad replied. "I'm going to rent a car and pick you up Monday night. We'll leave from Manhattan on Tuesday."

"That all sounds good except I'm a little confused," I said. "Bayville is so close to Maple Grove. Why don't you come and pick me up Tuesday, and we can just head right over from here?"

Dad laughed. "This is probably going to sound a little silly," he said. "But I thought it would feel more like a real vacation if you stayed over the night before we left. We could pack together, and you could help me decide what to bring. Then we could hit the road together on Tuesday."

"That doesn't sound silly to me at all," I said. "It sounds like a lot of fun. It's going to be great! Thanks, Dad."

"Love you, *mija*," he said.

"Love you, too," I replied, and hung up.

I climbed out of bed, and, still in my black T-shirt and shorts, went downstairs to tell Mom and Eddie the new plan.

"Everything okay with your dad?" Mom asked. She was standing at the counter, chopping up vegetables, and Eddie was on his laptop at the kitchen table.

"He's fine," I said. "We're going to his college reunion—well, he's going. I'm not going, but I'm going on the trip with him. We're going to stay with his old college friends."

"Toshi and Ayumi?" Mom asked.

I nodded. "That sounds right."

"They're very nice," Mom assured me. "I'm sure you'll have a good time."

"I hope so," I said as a I grabbed a box of cereal from the cabinet. "There's a beach there, so that will be nice."

Eddie looked up from his screen. "You're going to need to go shopping, Mia," he said. "You'll need a black bathing suit, a black beach towel, a black boogie board, black flip-flops . . ."

"Ha-ha," I said, but Eddie wasn't wrong. I had no interest in a boogie board, but all the other stuff—I definitely needed that! "Mom, can we go shopping this afternoon? I have Cupcake money."

Mom laughed and turned to my stepdad. "You nailed it, Ed," she said. "We can go after lunch—or breakfast, in your case. Also, Katie called too. You're invited for Chinese food and a movie tonight at the new house. She said she couldn't reach you on your cell phone."

"I was sleeping," I said, and Mom rolled her eyes.

"You're sleeping way too late these days, Mia," she said.

Eddie piped up. "Dan did the same thing when he was her age. It's because they're growing so much, and their bodies need the extra rest."

Eddie might be corny, but he's very chill and understanding, and I know I lucked out in the step-dad department. I nodded. "Yeah, what Eddie said."

Mom shook her head. "Abuela would have dumped a pot of ice water on me if I dared to sleep as late as you when I was your age," she said.

That sounded pretty horrible to me, but I didn't want to argue with Mom when I needed a ride to the mall.

"Well, I'm up now, and I can shower and be ready right away," I said. Then, for good measure, I hugged her. "Thanks for being the best mom ever."

"Thank you, Mia, but starting tomorrow I'm going to wake you up when Tiki and Milkshake wake up," she said. At the sound of their names, my two white Maltese dogs came running up to me, and I reached down and scratched the tops of their little heads. "I think you should walk them from now on, since you don't have any other activities this summer."

I stopped myself from protesting. In a few days

I'd be away with Dad, and he never cared how late I slept. I ate the last of my cereal and stood up.

"Showering now!" I said, and hurried upstairs. I hoped Mom might be willing to go to a couple of shops because I wasn't sure if I could find all my beach gear in black!

❖

We returned home from shopping at four o'clock, and I was really happy with what I scored. The beach stuff was on sale already, and I found a nice black racerback suit, black flip-flops with black appliqué flowers on them that I tried to take off but couldn't so I'd have to live with them, and a large black bath towel that I could use as a beach towel. I'd have to make my own black beach bag, but I figured I could do that myself.

"Put your stuff away, and then I'll take you to Katie's," Mom said.

"Okay!" I replied, and ran up the stairs to my room. Part of me was excited to see Katie, and part of me wondered if it might be different to be hanging out with Katie and her new family. Normally, it was just me, Katie, and her mom on Chinese food and movie nights. But now it would be the three of us, plus Mr. Green, my math teacher who is now Katie's stepdad. And then there's his daughter, Emily, who is now Katie's stepsister. So a lot has changed.

That made me a teeny bit nervous as I got out of the car in front of Katie's yellow house across from the park. Would we still have fun? Would it be awkward? Quiet? I wasn't sure what to expect.

The front door opened as soon as I stepped onto the porch.

"Mia's here!" Katie yelled at the top of her voice, and I relaxed a little. Things were definitely not going to be too quiet.

I waved good-bye to Mom, and Katie pulled me inside the house. "The food's here," she said. "I know you like chicken and broccoli, but we got *a lot* of dumplings this time. A lot! You have to eat some."

"Great," I said. "What movie are we watching?"

Katie bit her lip. "Well, um . . ."

I gave her a puzzled look, and she led me to the living room. The furniture was covered with sheets and pushed into the center of the room, and Katie's mom, Mr. Green, and Emily were all painting the walls.

"Mia, I'm so sorry!" Mrs. Brown said. "We thought we'd be done painting early this morning, but the day got away from us, and . . ."

"No problem—I like painting," I said.

"You're a sweetheart," Mrs. Brown said. She nodded to the other two painters. "Come on. Let's wash up and eat before the dumplings get cold."

I helped Katie set the dining room table and put out the food. Soon, we were all passing around the containers and filling our plates. Katie was right—there were *a lot* of dumplings. I picked up my chopsticks and popped one into my mouth.

"Mmmm, so good," I said.

"They're our new obsession," Katie said, and I like how she said "our," meaning her whole family.

"Mia, Katie says you're about to spend a week with your dad," Katie's mom said.

I nodded. "Yeah, but we're doing something different this time," I began, and told them about how we were going to stay with Dad's college friends.

Katie's eyes got wide. "You don't even know this girl, and you'll be stuck with her for a whole week!"

"Oh, Katie!" I laughed.

"What if she's a snob? What if she has no sense of humor?" Katie sounded panicked. "What if she is one of those girls who is always on a diet and SHE HATES CUPCAKES?"

I started to feel a little bit nervous again. "Well, Dad says everyone's cool," I said. "And we can leave

30

and go to a hotel if I don't like it there. Maybe I should just ask him to book a hotel now?"

"Maybe you should give it a try, Mia," Mr. Green said. "You might be surprised."

Emily nodded. "I worried about all those things before I met Katie," she said. "Well, not *all* those things. I knew that she liked cupcakes. But Katie turned out to be really nice."

"Aw, thanks, Em," Katie said. "I guess I shouldn't have been so negative. I'm sure this Tamiko girl will be perfectly fine."

"I hope so," Mia said.

Then Katie's eyes got big again. "What if it's the opposite? What if she's hilarious? And loves all the same things you love? What if she bakes amazing cupcakes, and you like her better than you like me?!"

"I can pretty much guarantee that I will never meet anybody I like better than you," I told her.

Katie smiled. "Everyone's saying the nicest things to me tonight! This is awesome."

Mr. Green pushed his chair back from the table. "If I eat another dumpling, I won't be able to lift up the paintbrush," he said.

"I'm ready to start the second coat," Mrs. Brown declared. "Katie and Emily, can you please clear the table and put the food away. Thanks so much!"

Emily jumped up. "On it!" she said.

I helped them, and soon, I was wielding a paintbrush and carefully painting the living room windowsill a pale yellow color. I couldn't imagine living in a room with *anything* painted yellow, but I didn't say that out loud. I tried to imagine the room with black walls, and that didn't seem right either. Then I imagined crisp white walls and black furniture—now *that* would look pretty cool.

"Mia's got such a steady hand," Katie's mom remarked. "Mia, what would we do without you?"

"What *will* we do without you when you're gone?" Katie asked.

"It's just a week," I said, but after our dinner conversation, I was starting to wonder why I'd agreed to the trip. A week could be a long time if you were stuck with somebody you didn't like. And for all I knew, Tamiko could be just as horrible as Katie had imagined!

CHAPTER 4

On the Road

"Bidi-bidi bom-bom! Bidi-bidi bom-bom!"

Dad was singing along to the song playing on the radio in the rental car. Alex Cruz is many things—handsome, a great dad, and a successful businessman. But he is not a very good singer.

"Dad! Stop!" I begged, but I was laughing.

"Come on, Mia, sing along," Dad urged. *"Bidi-bidi bidi-bidi bom-bom!"*

"This is a good song, but can't we just listen to Selena's voice?" I asked. "It's so pretty."

"I can't argue with that," Dad replied, and stopped singing and turned up the sound.

It was a beautiful, breezy summer Tuesday, and we'd been on the road for about two hours. Even though it was warm out, I'd convinced him to leave the windows open. I wanted to experience as much as I could—the wind on my face and the smells in the air.

"I'm so glad that the radio has a Selena channel," Dad said when the song was over.

"Yeah," I agreed. "But I don't get something. I mean, I understand why *I* like Selena, but why do you?"

"Why wouldn't I?" Dad replied.

"Well, she always sings about love and romance," I said. With a lot of practice, I'd gotten a lot better at learning Spanish over the last few months, and I finally understood what the pop star had been singing about.

"I like love and romance," Dad answered.

"Oh," I said. "I mean, it's just . . . you haven't had a girlfriend since Lynne."

"If I remember correctly, you weren't too fond of Lynne," Dad said.

"She was fine," I told him.

Dad turned to glance at me quickly. "What's up with this line of questioning, *mija*?"

"I guess I've just been thinking about you since Katie's mom got married," I told him. "She has Mr. Green, and Mom married Eddie, but you don't have anybody. Are you sad?"

"You don't need to be with somebody to be happy, Mia," Dad said. "I'm fine."

"But wouldn't it be nice to have a girlfriend?" I asked. "You could create a profile on a dating site. There are a lot out there."

Dad started to shake his head. "No way. That's not for me. I believe in fate. If the right woman is out there for me, I'm going to meet her. I'll know her when I see her."

I raised an eyebrow. "Wow, that's pretty romantic. Okay, I get why you like Selena now."

Dad laughed.

After a few minutes, he looked at his watch, then back at the road, and whistled. "Traffic is going to be pretty bad right about now," he said. "What do you say we stop at a diner for a quick burger to kill some time? Then hopefully the traffic will have eased up a bit when we start traveling again."

I nodded and patted my belly. "Sounds good," I said. "I could eat!"

Dad grinned. "I know the perfect place," he said. "They make their fries thin and crispy, just the way you like them—and not greasy at all."

My stomach started growling the minute he said "fries," and suddenly I was starving.

❀

Dad stopped the car in front of a restaurant called the Good Stuff Diner. When we sat down, I snapped a pic of the menu cover and sent it to Katie, Alexis, and Emma.

Alexis wrote: Make sure to check out their dessert menu and see if they have cupcakes.

That was Alexis for you, always thinking about the cupcake business.

"Mia, I hope you won't be on your phone when we eat with the Satos," Dad said.

"I won't. I'm not rude," I said.

Dad raised an eyebrow.

"It's just you and me, and we've been in the car a really long time," I protested. "Besides, you got on your phone as soon as we sat down."

"That was for work," Dad argued.

"Ha!" I said. "Same thing."

"Not at all," Dad protested, and then he gave the server our food order.

Dad leaned back in his chair and smiled. "It will be nice to see Toshi again," he said. "It's been a long time. We were such good friends in college. He sort of took me under his wing. He was so outgoing and popular, and I was pretty shy."

That surprised me. My dad was always so lively and fun. All my friends loved him.

"You ... shy?" I said. "I find that hard to believe."

"It's true!" Dad protested. "But like I said, Toshi took me everywhere with him, and after a while I just followed his lead. I would always get flustered and nervous around new people, especially girls! But Toshi showed me how to just relax and be myself, to smile a lot and listen a lot and ask questions and pay compliments. After a while I wondered what I was ever afraid of, meeting new people was easy ... and fun!"

❀

I ordered a hamburger, French fries, and a vanilla shake. When the waitress set my plate down everything looked so yummy I snapped another photo for the girls.

Jelly! Katie texted. I need those fries in my belly!

Dad's story about meeting new people reminded me of his promise. "So, once we get to the Satos, if I don't like it there we can leave and go to a hotel?" I said. I wanted to make sure Dad hadn't forgotten his promise.

"Yes, if you're truly miserable," Dad replied. "But I think it will be good for you to meet some new people, Mia. In a few years you'll be thinking of going to college, and you'll be meeting lots of new people there. I don't want you to waste time being shy or nervous like I was! So maybe you should try to embrace this experience."

"I already have college planned out," I told him. "Katie and I are going to go to the same school, and we're going to be roommates. And when we graduate we're going to get an apartment together in the city. So I won't have to meet any new people unless I want to."

Dad smiled. "It's nice to have plans and dreams, but sometimes plans change, *mija*," he said. "Just keep yourself open to new ideas and new people."

It was my turn to raise an eyebrow at him. "But *you're* not trying to meet new people. You just said so in the car."

"That's different," Dad said.

I shook my head. "That can't be your answer for everything!"

Then our server came back to the table.

"How is everything?" she asked with a smile. Her blond hair was pulled back in a neat bun, and she had friendly blue eyes. Her name tag read KAYLIN.

"Delicious," I replied.

"Yes—I remembered the food here was good. I ate here once before," Dad answered, and smiled at her.

"Well, I hope you're enjoying your visit," Kaylin said.

"We're just passing through," Dad told her. "I'm on my way to my college reunion, with my daughter."

"How sweet! What a fun thing to do together," Kaylin said. "Well, you just let me know if you need anything else. You have to have the dessert here. The key lime pie is amazing."

Kaylin left, and I leaned across the table. "She's so nice! Why don't you ask her out?"

Dad laughed.

"You are too much, Mia," Dad said. "How about this: You stay out of my love life, and I'll stay out of yours."

"I don't have one," I said. It was true. I'd had a crush on Chris Howard for a while, but then he started liking somebody else, and . . .

I must have had a troubled look on my face as I thought about it because Dad said, "Sore subject, I see. It's tough being your age. You're too young to be in love, or date, but having a crush on someone can feel so huge, and you have all of these confusing feelings. . . ."

"All right! I won't bug you about dating anymore, I promise," I told him.

39

Dad grinned. "I'm glad we're on the same page."

We listened to Kaylin's advice and got the key lime pie for dessert, and it was amazing! I texted a picture of it to the Cupcake Girls.

Key lime cupcakes?

Yes!! Alexis replied. Vanilla cupcake, key lime frosting, graham cracker crumble on top!

❀

When we finished eating. Dad stood up and stretched.

"We'd better hit the road," he said. "We're still at least an hour from Bayville, if the traffic isn't too bad."

"Another hour!" I complained.

"Take a nap," Dad suggested.

"I'm not sleepy," I said.

"Then . . . you can pick the music," he said.

I did end up napping after all. I woke up as we pulled into a rest stop. So I was wide awake as we got closer and closer to Bayville. I looked down at the outfit I had picked to meet the Satos. I put on a black sleeveless tank dress and a black choker with a heart dangling from it. Black wedge sandals completed the look, and I had pulled my hair back into a high ponytail.

Would the Satos be nice? Would Tamiko be the

cupcake-hating monster Katie imagined? Normally, I'm not shy about meeting new people, but this was different. We'd go from meeting one another to living together.

Still, I was more excited than nervous, even before we saw the WELCOME TO BAYVILLE sign. To the right was the beach and the ocean glittering in the distance. To the left was a cute downtown with shops and restaurants. I smelled food cooking and saw an open-air mall with food trucks inside.

"A food truck court!" I said. "Oh wow, Katie would love it here!"

Dad turned away from the shopping area, and we drove down some streets with cute little beach cottages painted white, with accents in pretty colors like pink, turquoise, and yellow. Then the town got less beachy and more suburban, with apartment buildings, grocery stores, a school, and a hospital.

After that we entered a section of Bayville with big old houses. No two were alike, but they all had porches and turrets and wood shingles. Some had peeling paint, and some looked like they had just been painted. It wasn't as cute as the beach neighborhood, but the streets were lined with pretty trees, and lots of the homes had flowers planted in front of them.

Dad pulled into the driveway of a white house, with a neat front lawn and four bicycles in a rack on the side. As I pulled open the sun visor to check my hair in the mirror, I heard a loud voice.

"Alex! You're here!"

A woman my dad's age came running down the front steps toward us. She had a cute shoulder-length haircut and wore a gray T-shirt, jeans, and vintage sneakers. I immediately got a cool vibe from her.

Dad got out of the car first. "Ayumi!" He gave her a hug. Then her husband, who was taller than my dad, caught up to them and gave my dad a very firm handshake.

"Good to see you, Alex. Hope you didn't have too much traffic," he said.

"Some, but we had a great ride, Toshi," my dad replied. I had emerged from the car by then, and Dad motioned to me. "This is my daughter, Mia."

"Nice to meet you," I said.

"Oh, Alex, she's gorgeous!" Mrs. Sato said. Then she turned toward the house. "Tamiko! Our guests are here!"

I heard a voice from the window. "ONE MINUTE! I can't just leave my glue gun plugged in!"

42

Glue gun? Was Tamiko one of those crafty girls who made scrapbooks and stuff?

"TAMIKO!" Mrs. Sato yelled again, and a few seconds later, a girl came bounding out of the house. Her hair was in a ponytail, like mine, and cute cherry earrings dangled from her ears. She wore a blue, box-cut top over a flouncy red skirt with white polka dots, and white sneakers decorated with what looked like tiny plastic toys.

She stopped and stared at me, and we both didn't say anything for a few seconds. Then, at the same time, we both blurted out, "I LOVE YOUR OUTFIT!"

CHAPTER 5

Tamiko Is Loud, Stylish, and Cool!

Our parents laughed.

"I told you they had a lot in common," my dad said to Mrs. Sato.

"Tamiko, why don't you take Mia up to your room," Mrs. Sato said. "She probably wants to freshen up from her trip."

"What does 'freshen up' even mean?" Tamiko asked. "That is such an old person thing to say."

Mrs. Sato sighed. "Mia, please feel free to unpack, use the bathroom, get some water," she said. Then she looked at Tamiko. "Was that clearer?"

"Perfect!" Tamiko replied. "Come on, Mia."

I wasn't exactly sure to make of this highly fashionable, loud, cute girl who spoke so casually to her mom. But I knew I wanted to find out more. I got my bags out of the trunk and followed her inside and up the stairs.

"We set up a futon for you in my customization room," Tamiko said as we entered her bedroom. "You know, for privacy."

"Customization room?" I asked, looking around. Tamiko's bedroom was just as colorful as she was, with posters and pictures from magazines all over the walls, and fuzzy pillows in every shade of the rainbow on her bed. Tamiko opened the doors and led me into a smaller side room.

"Wow, it's like you have your own apartment here," I said, looking around. This room definitely looked like a crafty space, with plastic bins holding stuff like patches, jars of paint, and spools of thread. A turquoise-painted hutch held more supplies. And pillows and blankets were piled on a folded-up futon on the back wall.

"I usually keep my sewing machine on a table in here, but we had to take it out so you would fit," Tamiko said.

Is she trying to make me feel bad or just being really honest? I wondered. I was starting to get the idea that Tamiko just said whatever she was feeling.

"I sew too," I said. "And I also keep my machine in my bedroom. It would be awesome to have an extra room like this the way you do."You're lucky!

"Yeah, I'm pretty lucky," Tamiko admitted. "It's a good thing my parents never decided to give me a baby brother or baby sister, or I'd be out of luck."

"I'm an only child," I told her. "Unless you count my stepbrother, Dan."

"Is Dan an obnoxious toddler?" she asked.

I laughed. "No, he's a sophomore. And not obnoxious. Well, mostly."

"My brother, Kai, is a sophomore too," Tamiko said. "And he's not obnoxious either. I'm the obnoxious one in the family."

I laughed, and then across the room, I spotted her open closet, which was filled with colorful clothes.

"Is that a tutu?" I asked, spotting a poof of lavender tulle among the other clothes. "I love them, but I've never had the guts to pull one off."

Tamiko walked to the closet and pulled it out. "They're superfun to wear. They make you feel like a magical fairy or something. But also, they photograph great. I put my friend Allie in this, and it got so many likes on my blog."

"You have a blog?" I asked her.

She nodded. *Tamiko's Take.* She grabbed a tablet from the top of her dresser, turned it on, and handed it to me. It was impressive.

I scrolled through the screen, looking at each of her blog posts. One post was about this all-girl rock band wearing really cute and fun clothes. There were other posts featuring other girls our age. And there was a girl in the tutu, with freckles and light brown hair, holding an ice-cream cone with ice cream the same lavender color as the tutu.

"This is so cool," I said. "Are these your friends? And do you style all the outfits yourself?"

Tamiko nodded. "I make some of them, too."

"I made my friend Katie's dress for her mom's wedding!" I said, and took out my phone and showed her a photo of Katie wearing what I'd made. The soft pink dress had fluttery sleeves and tiny roses sewn into the skirt.

"Whoa," Tamiko said. "Did you sew in all those roses by hand?"

I nodded. "Yes. It took a long time, but Katie's my best friend, so I didn't mind."

"It's really nice," Tamiko said, and then she glanced over at the closet. "Do you have anything you need to hang up in my closet? I was supposed to make room for you, but . . ."

"Maybe just the dress that I brought," I said. I carried my bags back into the side room and zipped open my big duffel bag. Tamiko stood in the door-way and watched, and I searched for the black sun dress I wanted to hang up.

"Did your father tell you there was going to be a funeral?" she asked.

"Not you too!" I said. "Everybody's been giving me a hard time about wearing all black. I mean, has no one ever heard of Coco Chanel?"

"Good point," Tamiko said. "Hey, so if you want to do that freshening up thing, I'll meet you down-stairs."

"Sure, thanks," I said.

After I unpacked and splashed some water on my face, I went downstairs and heard voices com-ing from the backyard. I followed the sound and found Tamiko there with her parents, my dad, and a boy who I guessed was her brother.

"Hi, Mia. I'm Kai," he said, walking up to me and smiling. "Tamiko's brother. I hope she's being nice to you."

"Hey!" Tamiko shouted. "I'm being really nice. Mia will back me up."

I nodded. "Tamiko is the perfect hostess," I said.

"You know it," Tamiko replied, and she and I moved over to a table shaded by an umbrella.

Tamiko's dad was cooking chicken on a grill,

and Dad and Mrs. Sato were standing next to him, talking and laughing. They were listening to music on a speaker that sounded like I think what you would call punk rock—from their college days, I guessed. Dad looked so happy.

Then Tamiko and I started talking about all kinds of stuff—her school, my school; her friends, my friends. Then she scrolled through her tablet and I scrolled through my phone, looking for outfits we liked.

Before we knew it, it was time for dinner, and I was good and hungry. We sat down at the dining room table inside for a meal of grilled chicken, cold Japanese noodles, and cucumber salad.

"Everything is so delicious," I announced. "My friend Katie would love all of this. She's going to be a chef someday."

"I heard about your cupcake business, Mia," Mrs. Sato said. "Are you going to be a chef too?"

I shook my head. " I'm going to study fashion design. I already take classes in the city."

Tamiko sighed. "I wish I could take fashion classes too." Then she brightened. "Hey, maybe I could take a class when we go to Tokyo!"

"You're going to Tokyo?" I asked.

Next to Paris, Tokyo was a place I dreamed of

visiting because of the amazing fashion scene there.

"We go every summer, to visit my grandfather," Tamiko replied.

"That's so cool. You must get so many inspirations there," I said, and then we started talking about the best shopping districts in Tokyo.

Mrs. Sato looked at my dad. "It's so weird, Alex! It's like you and Sara had the same kid we did," she said.

"They do seem to be a lot alike," my dad agreed. "Although Tamiko might be a little more colorful than Mia."

"Black *is* a color," I reminded him, and then ignored him and continued to talk to Tamiko. I wouldn't say we were twins, exactly, but it *was* kind of weird how much we had in common.

Mrs. Sato interrupted us. "Tamiko, maybe Mia would like to go shopping with us for your dress for the Japan Society dinner."

"I would love to do that," I said.

Tamiko frowned. "But I have an outfit," she said.

Mrs. Sato sighed. "Tamiko, we have gone over this," she said. "You cannot wear polka-dot leggings to this dinner."

"But I'm wearing them with a dress," Tamiko replied. "They complete the look. Wait till you see it all together. It's fantastic!" She turned to me. "Mia will back me up. I'll show her what I'm wearing, and she'll tell you that it's fashion."

"Well . . . um . . . I . . ." I didn't want to get between Tamiko and her mom in an argument.

"We'll discuss this later, Tamiko," Mrs. Sato said, and Tamiko rolled her eyes.

Kai spoke up. "Maybe now would be a good time to go over the schedule for the next few days," he said. "I've got the itinerary plotted out hour by hour."

"Boring," Tamiko muttered.

I smiled at him. "You remind me of my friend Alexis," I said. "She loves a good schedule."

"She sounds pretty smart," Kai said. "Anyway, here are the main events: the weather is going to be great for the beach tomorrow. Thursday and Friday are a good days to go shopping and the beach. And Saturday is the reunion, so I've got some ideas for things that Tamiko, Mia, and I can do together. Sunday is the only day I don't have an exact plan for, since Tamiko will be working at Molly's all day."

"What's Molly's?" I asked.

"My friend Allie's mom owns an ice-cream shop, with all homemade ice cream," Tamiko explained. "I am the company's social media director, and every Sunday my friends Allie, Sierra, and I help out at the shop. We're the Sundae Sisters."

"That sounds like fun," I said.

"I was thinking we could go there after dinner," Mr. Sato said. "Unless you and Mia are tired, Alex."

Dad looked at me, and I shook my head. "I'm not tired. I would love to see the shop!"

We cleared off the table, and then Dad and I got in the rental car and followed the Satos back into the cute little downtown area we'd driven through to get to their house. The streets were a lot more crowded now that everyone was done with the beach, and we had to park in a lot a few blocks away from the shop. As we walked I had to admit that I *did* feel tired. But I was really excited to try the ice cream and meet Tamiko's friend Allie.

There was a line out the door when we got to Molly's, but it was moving quickly, and it gave me time to peek inside. The seats had aqua-and-white–striped cushions that matched the awnings outside. The black-and-white–checkered floor gave the whole place a retro feel, and cute touches like light fixtures that looked like ice-cream cones made it look really fun.

Tamiko stepped out of the line and started taking pictures with her cell phone. "This will make a great post for Molly's page," she remarked.

When we stepped into the shop, I was able to read the ice-cream board. There were so many flavors! Some of them sounded really unique: Hokeypokey Honeycomb, Balsamic Strawberry, St. Louis Butter Cake.

"Tamiko, which flavor should I try?" I asked.

"How about a Mermaid Sundae?" she suggested. "It's one of our most popular creations."

"I don't think I could eat a whole sundae right now," I replied. "Maybe just a cone?"

Tamiko looked thoughtful. "Then . . . maybe try the Peach Pie. Fresh local peaches with a graham cracker swirl. It's only available when peaches are in season."

"That sounds good," I said.

We stepped up to the counter, where two college-age kids were taking orders. With them was the girl in the tutu from Tamiko's blog.

"Allie!" Tamiko called out. "This is Mia, the one I was telling you about."

Allie smiled at me. "It's nice to meet you."

"We had nothing to worry about. She's really cool," Tamiko said, and I raised my eyebrows.

"Tamiko!" Allie scolded.

"It's okay," I said. "My friends and I were worried

about Tamiko too, but she is pretty cool."

"How dare you!" Tamiko teased. Then she nodded to Allie. "One cone with a scoop of Coca Mocha, and another with a scoop of Peach Pie, please. And my parents are paying." She nodded back to them.

"Coming up," Allie said. She scooped out my ice cream, and then I saw her move over to the bin of rainbow sprinkles.

"No sprinkles for me, thanks," I said.

"But you have to," Tamiko protested. "It's a shop tradition."

How could I argue? "All right. Sprinkles," I said.

Allie dipped the cone into the sprinkles and handed it to me. "Enjoy your sprinkle of happy," she said, and I couldn't help smiling. I mean, you *have* to smile when you're holding an ice-cream cone covered with colorful sprinkles, don't you?

There were no seats in the shop, so we ate our ice cream as we strolled around downtown. Tamiko was chatting about the shops and what you could find in each of them, but the ice cream was so delicious, I wasn't paying attention.

"This is really amazing!" I said as I crunched down on the crispy cone. "I swear it's the best I've ever tasted!"

"Can I use that on social media?" Tamiko asked. "'Girl from NYC says Molly's ice cream is the best she's ever tasted!'"

I laughed. "You're kidding, right?"

"Yes," Tamiko replied. "But I'm glad you like it. You'll have to try all the flavors before you leave."

Then we all piled back into our cars and drove back to the Satos.

When we got back to the house, I showered and crashed on the futon in Tamiko's little craft room. My phone buzzed with a text from Katie.

How is it? Is Tamiko nice? Are you having fun?

So far, so good! I wrote back.

I'm so glad! I miss you already! Katie texted with a bunch of hearts.

Miss U 2, I replied, and then turned off my phone and fell into an exhausted sleep.

CHAPTER 6

Beach Day

$\mathcal{K}$ai had us scheduled to head to the beach at nine a.m. the next morning. I would have loved to sleep until noon, but I knew I had to go along with the game plan. Besides, I was kind of eager to see the beach in Bayville.

Tamiko watched me with interest as I packed up my black beach bag with a black towel, black coverup, and black hairbrush while wearing a black T-shirt and shorts over my black bathing suit, with black flip-flops.

"It's impressive, really," Tamiko said. "I mean, when you commit, you really commit." Over her suit, she wore a cute, sleeveless turquoise jersey dress with a Japanese kanji pattern.

"Thanks?" I replied, not sure if she meant that

as a compliment. But she was right. It wasn't easy finding everything I wanted in black.

We had to take two cars again and parked near the beach. The Satos had a bunch of beach stuff: a beach canopy; beach chairs; and a big white cooler on wheels that Kai informed us was packed with sandwiches he'd made himself.

"Your brother is so nice," I told Tamiko as we walked ahead of everyone. "Dan would never make a schedule for us, and I can't imagine him making us sandwiches!"

"Don't be too impressed," Tamiko said. "I mean, yeah, he's generally nice, but he's taking a business hospitality course this summer so it will look good on his college applications. All this is basically extra credit."

I glanced back at Kai, who was pulling the cooler down the sidewalk.

"Well, I'm sure he'll get an A plus," I told Tamiko.

Dad was walking with Tamiko's parents, talking away—it seemed like they hadn't stopped talking since we got here. I'd kind of missed Dad checking in with me before bed last night, and that made me feel a little bit silly.

You're not a little kid, Mia! I reminded myself.

Soon we reached the boardwalk, which was

lined with brightly painted vacation houses. We walked to the nearest beach entrance, and then I felt my feet sink into the sand. A slight breeze was blowing, and seagulls swooped against the bright blue sky. Umbrellas and beach towels dotted the bright sand.

Kai led us to "the perfect spot," and we set up the beach canopy and the chairs. I kicked off my flip-flops.

"Is everybody sunscreened?" Mrs. Sato asked.

"We did it back at the house," Tamiko replied, and her mom nodded.

"All right. But we're reapplying every thirty minutes. I've got the spray stuff here," she said.

Tamiko turned to me. "We should go to the water now. The waves are just right."

"Sure," I said, and followed her to the water's edge. I took a few cautious steps into the almost-too-cold water, but Tamiko charged right in, ran several feet, and then dove into the oncoming wave.

She emerged, grinning with her hair dripping. "Come on in!" she urged.

I froze. When Dad had mentioned coming to the beach, I'd thought about collecting seashells, napping on a beach blanket, that kind of thing. I've never done any actual ocean swimming.

"I—I know how to swim, but I don't really know how to swim in the ocean," I confessed.

She splashed toward me and took my hand. "It's easy. When a wave comes, you just dive under it and swim like you're swimming underwater. The waves aren't too strong now. You'll be fine."

"Okay," I said, and looked back at the lifeguard in the tall chair for reassurance. She looked strong, with pretty impressive biceps, and I figured she could rescue me if I totally failed.

I walked up to Tamiko, shivering as the water crept up above my knees. A small wave was rolling toward us.

"Oh, you might want to hold your nose," Tamiko said.

"What do you—"

Whoosh! The wave lapped over us, and I could feel the cold water go up my nose. I pushed forward with my arms and kicked, and as the wave receded, I found my footing on the sandy ocean floor. Then I shook my head, splattering water drops everywhere like my dogs do when I give them a bath.

"How was it?" Tamiko asked me.

"Not bad," I lied.

"If we get just a little bit ahead of where the waves break, we can float," Tamiko said. "Come on."

She swam out a few more yards, and I followed. I could see the buoys in the distance, marking the spot where it was too dangerous to go ahead. We were still far behind them.

Tamiko leaned back in the water, flattening her body. "Now float."

I copied her and was surprised that the water held me up. I had to paddle a little to stay afloat, but it was pretty nice and relaxing.

"Tell me more about your cupcake business," Tamiko said. "You and your friends run it yourselves? You don't work for anybody?"

I shook my head. "We are the owners and operators. My friend Alexis is a business genius like your brother, so she does all the accounting, which I think is the hardest part. But everyone bakes and comes up with new cupcake flavors and decorations."

"We do that too, but with ice cream," Tamiko remarked. "New sundaes are always big sellers because some customers just want to try something different every time."

Then we heard a voice call from the shore.

"Tamiiiiiikoooooooooooo!"

Tamiko raised her head. "Sierra!" She paddled forward, and when she could stand, splashed through the water to the shore. She seemed excited.

I followed her, curious. The girl on the sand had long, curly brown hair and wore a purple flowery two-piece suit. Then it clicked: I had seen her in the photo of Tamiko's blog. She was the singer in that all-girl rock band.

Tamiko hugged her and then nodded toward me. "Sierra, this is the supercool Mia, who wears black all the time but says she isn't goth. And, Mia, this is Sierra, my gorgeous friend with the voice of an angel and who also works at the ice-cream shop with me and Allie."

"Hey," I said.

Sierra smiled. "Hey. You both didn't have to get out of the water on my account."

"Want to swim?" Tamiko asked.

"I just want to go in up to my knees," Sierra replied. "I'm volunteering at the animal shelter later, and I don't want my hair to get wet because I won't have time to fix it before I go."

"Yeah, because everyone knows that adorable puppies and kittens are so judgmental," Tamiko teased.

"Well, there are people there, too, you know," Sierra reminded her, and we waded back into the water.

"Tamiko showed me the photo shoot she did of you and your band," I said. "My stepbrother and cousin are in a band, but they mostly just scream and play their instruments extra loud."

Sierra laughed. "Reagan—she writes most of our songs—says we're a rock band, but I think we have more of a modern sound. And I don't scream when I sing."

Then she turned to Tamiko. "Oh, I almost forgot to tell you. Connor Jackson was riding his bicycle past his house last night, and he almost got hit by a car! I saw the whole thing. But when he swerved to miss it, he hit a tree."

"Wow! Is he okay?" Tamiko asked.

"My mom called an ambulance for him, and he posted a picture of himself later with a cast on his wrist," Sierra said. "And then Kerry Phan commented underneath it with a heart!"

Tamiko gasped. "Kerry? But she's so nice, and Connor is so—"

"I know, I know!" Sierra said, and they both started laughing.

Then they started to talk about more kids from their school, and I felt a little left out.

"I'm going to go back to the canopy" I said.

"Sure," Tamiko replied, and kept talking to

Sierra. She didn't seem the least bit concerned that I was leaving.

I slowly made my way back to the shore, wishing I had Katie or Emma or Alexis with me. *Maybe the Cupcake Club needs to take a beach field trip,* I thought. *We work together a lot, but we don't do enough fun things together.*

Then a flash of white at my feet caught my eye, and I bent down to see what it was. It was a scallop shell, streaked with orange, and I liked how pretty it was, so I picked it up. Then another shell caught my eye, and I bent down to get that one too. This one had a pearly look on the inside.

I glanced back at Tamiko and Sierra. Still chatting. I shaded my eyes and saw Dad talking with the Satos over at the canopy Kai was nowhere in sight.

I might as well look for more shells, I thought, and kept my head down, trying to spot another one. I took a few more steps and—

"Whoa!"

I'd bumped right into someone! A boy wearing a colorful tie-dye shirt and blue swimming trunks. He was about my height, with curly brown hair and dark eyes.

"Sorry," I said, but he didn't look upset. He was smiling.

"It's okay," he said, and then bent down and picked up a shell and handed it to me. "Is that what you were looking for?"

"Yes—I mean, I—I guess," I stammered. "I'm Mia." *Why had I said that?*

"Aaron," he replied. He hesitated for a minute, and neither one of us said anything more. He nodded and kept walking.

"Thanks for the shell!" I called after him, and he turned back and smiled.

I walked ahead quickly, back to the canopy, feeling awkward. *Thanks for the shell?* He'd seemed perfectly nice, like someone I could have had a conversation with.

I guess I'm just destined to be alone today. I stretched out on my beach towel under the canopy, closed my eyes, and drifted off to sleep.

Splashes of cold water woke me up a short while later, and I opened my eyes to see Tamiko and Sierra under the canopy, both with wet hair.

"I convinced Sierra to swim," Tamiko announced. "You should have come with us."

"I might if you had asked me," I replied, trying not to sound annoyed.

"We didn't want to wake you," Sierra said.

I sat up. Dad and the rest of Tamiko's family were

walking back from the water, all wet from swimming. Kai toweled himself off and then moved to the cooler.

"Time for lunch!" he announced. "The salt air makes me so hungry!"

"I've got to run," Sierra said. "But thanks, anyway!"

She packed up her beach bag, said good-bye to everybody, and left, while Kai set up the food on a picnic blanket under the tent. Curious seagulls hopped around on the sand next to us.

"Don't feed them!" Mr. Sato warned. "They won't leave us alone if you do."

"I made turkey rollups," Kai informed us. "And there are carrot sticks, grapes, oatmeal cookies, and a thermos of lemonade."

"You outdid yourself, Kai," Mrs. Sato said.

"Yeah, this looks awesome," I agreed, and grabbed some food and brought it back to my beach towel to eat.

Kai took his cell phone from his pocket. "If nobody minds, I'm going to take some pictures for my class."

"Go for it," Tamiko said. She held the sandwich and made a goofy fake smile. "This is the best sandwich in the whole wide world!"

"You can just act natural, Tamiko," Kai said.

"When have I ever acted natural?" Tamiko shot back.

"Kai, I think we might need to veer off schedule a bit this afternoon," his mom said. "It's going to be really hot soon, and I think we'd all be better off chilling out in the AC. Plus, us grown-ups have some work we have to get done."

"That's fine with me," I chimed in. Chilling out sounded like exactly what I wanted to do. Plus maybe sleep some more.

Everyone agreed, so we packed up our gear and headed back to the cars. When we got to the house, I took a nice cool shower and changed into a black layered tank top and my favorite skirt I'd brought; a short, flouncy one. I'd brought it in case we went out to dinner, but I felt like wearing it, and it was perfect for a hot day.

When I walked back into Tamiko's room, she was setting up a folding table next to her bed, and there was an old-looking sewing machine on the floor.

"Oh, hey," she said. "I need to finish a project I've been working on. Do you mind?"

"No, go ahead," I said.

"Normally I'd work in my Customization

Room, but your futon's in there. . . ." Her voice trailed off. I started to feel a little uncomfortable.

"Do you need me to move out of there?" I asked her. I got the definite feeling that Tamiko wasn't thrilled about having her space invaded.

"No, this should work," she said, and placed the machine on the table and plugged it into the wall.

I went into the little room and sat on the futon. I took out my phone and texted Katie.

What's up?

Nothing. It's boring here without you, Katie replied.

Same. Wish u were here, I typed.

Katie responded with a bunch of crying faces and hearts, and we didn't have too much to say to each other after that. I scrolled on my phone for a while, and then I heard the sound of Tamiko's machine.

Curious, I peered into the bedroom to see what she was making. I saw two sleeves of a denim jacket on the floor, and Tamiko was sewing the body of the jacket.

"Are you turning that jacket into a vest?" I asked over the sound of the machine, and Tamiko nodded.

I walked over to get a better look.

"It's for my next blog shoot," she said. "I found this in a thrift shop. The jacket is kind of dated, but I think I can do something fresh with the vest."

She slid the vest out from under the machine and picked up what looked like a thick, orange marker.

"Is that a fabric marker?" I asked.

She shook her head. "No, it's a bleach pen. You know how bleach removes color from fabric? With a pen, you can draw with it, and you get white designs on any color."

"I've seen that, but I've never tried it," I told her. "What kind of design are you going to do?"

Tamiko uncapped the pen. "I'm not sure," she said. "I was thinking of words on the back, but I'm not sure what to write. I was thinking, maybe 'GOAT'—you know, 'Greatest of All Time.'"

I laughed. "That's pretty good," I said. "Or what about 'YOLO'! You know, 'You Only Live Once'? That could be funny."

"Yeah, something like that," Tamiko said. "Or maybe just a pattern, but I couldn't find the right shape."

I started searching on my phone. "I saw this cool *x* pattern on one of the runway collections this spring. Hold on."

I found the photo I was looking for and showed it to Tamiko. "Maybe something like this?"

"YES!" she yelled, waving her arms excitedly. Then her face fell, and I wasn't sure why—until I saw that she was looking at my skirt.

The bleach pen in her hand had accidentally streaked my black skirt! Now there was a curvy white line going across the front. It was ruined!

"Mia, I am so sorry!" Tamiko said.

"It's okay," I told her, but it didn't feel okay. In fact, I felt like crying all of a sudden, but I held back the tears. "I'm just going to go change."

I went back into the smaller room and changed into a pair of black shorts, stuffing the skirt into my bag. I knew that Tamiko was trying to be nice, and the bleach thing wasn't really her fault, but this whole situation of spending time with a stranger was starting to get on my nerves!

CHAPTER 7

Baking with Tamiko

I texted my dad.

Can we do something just the two of us tomorrow?

He replied quickly. You okay? We can go to a hotel.

I thought about how nice the Satos were being and how it might hurt their feelings if we suddenly left.

No hotel, I replied. But just you and me 2morrow morning, okay?

You got it! Dad replied. Love you!

After that, I was kind of quiet for the rest of the night. Dad took us out to dinner at a restaurant specializing in Southern food. It would have been the perfect place for me to wear my skirt, but instead, I had to wear my black sleeveless jersey dress, which is cute, but not as cute as the skirt. I sat between

Dad and Kai and didn't talk to Tamiko much at all. In fact, I didn't talk to anybody much at all. Even though my chicken and waffles were tasty (Katie had told me to order them, after I texted her the restaurant menu), I could not shake my meh mood.

I fell asleep early and woke up before nine the next morning. Dad took me out to breakfast at a cute little doughnut shop, and we walked around the area of town with all the shops.

"Thanks for doing this with me," I told him as we browsed in a store selling postcards, seashells, and fancy lotions and soaps.

"It's nice to have time alone with you," Dad replied. "Besides, I'm sure the Satos might need a break from us too."

That hadn't occurred to me, but I guessed Dad was right. I tried to imagine Tamiko sharing my room with me for a few days, and had to admit that it wouldn't be easy.

I bought some necklaces to bring back to Katie, Emma, and Alexis—skinny silver chains with a pearly pink shell dangling from the end. Then Dad and I moved on to the next store—a candy store, filled with everything from saltwater taffy to chocolates shaped like dolphins.

"I'm going to put together a box of candy for

back home," I told Dad. I knew Mom, Eddie, and Dan would really like that. I wandered over to a case with the differently shaped chocolates, and leaned in to look inside.

Some butterflies for Mom, I thought. *And some cute dogs for Eddie.* I looked to see if they had a guitar-shaped chocolate I could pick out for Dan. I turned my head—and found myself looking into the face of a cute boy with curly hair and dark eyes. It was Aaron, the boy I'd met on the beach yesterday!

"Hi, Aaron," I said, straightening up.

"Oh, wow, Mia, you remember me?" he asked.

"Well, you're easy to recognize," I said, pointing to his tie-dyed shirt. "You're wearing the same clothes as yesterday."

He laughed. "It's a totally different shirt. I could say the same about you, dressed all in black."

"I guess you could," I replied.

"So, are you going to the beach today?" he asked.

"I'm not sure," I said. "We're here for my dad's college reunion and are staying with his friends. They've been coming up with stuff to do."

"Can I help you?"

The teenage girl behind the counter was looking at us impatiently.

"Oh, yes, please," I said. "Can I start with three butterflies?"

The girl picked up a little white box and started adding the candy. Then my dad walked up.

"Everything here looks so good!" he said.

Aaron waved. "Well, um, see you, Mia," he said, and then disappeared behind the saltwater taffy display.

Dad raised an eyebrow. "Who was that?"

I shrugged. "Just some boy I met on the beach yesterday." I braced myself for more questions, but Dad didn't go there. Instead, he bent down to look at the chocolates.

"We should get some for the Satos," he said, and after I filled my box to bring home, we filled another box for them.

We went to a few more shops after that, and I found a cute black tank top and a black cross-body bag to add to my wardrobe. Then Dad said it was time to go back to the Satos for lunch.

"What are we doing the rest of the day?" I asked.

Dad shrugged. "I'm not sure. I guess whatever Kai has scheduled for us," he said with a chuckle.

I wondered how things were going to be with me and Tamiko when we got back to the Satos' house. I'd kind of stopped being chatty with her

73

after my skirt got ruined, which wasn't even her fault. I wouldn't blame her if she didn't want to hang out with me.

But when we got to the front door, it opened before we could ring the bell. Tamiko ran out and grabbed me by the arm.

"Upstairs!" she commanded. "I've got something to show you."

By now I was used to Tamiko's way of saying things, so I was excited and not insulted. When we got to her room, she waved her arm at my skirt, which was displayed on her bed. The bleach streak was gone!

"I dyed it black," she said. "It's as good as new."

I picked up the skirt. What a really nice thing for her to do! "Tamiko, thank you! You didn't have to do that."

"Yes I did! I ruined your skirt. Tamiko replied.

"It was an accident," I said. "But thanks. And anyway, I thought what you were doing with the bleach pen was really cool. I'd like to try it out sometime."

"Sure! Maybe after we eat?" Tamiko suggested. "I think Kai has us scheduled for free time." She shook her head, laughing.

"Sounds good," I said, and we headed back

downstairs to eat lunch. I realized I was starving.

As we munched on sandwiches and potato salad, Tamiko's mom laid out some ideas for how we should use our free time.

"I was thinking tonight, when it's cooler, we could bake some cupcakes together," she said. "Mia, maybe you could show us one of your favorite recipes?"

"Sure," I said, and started thinking about what might be fun to make, and what I really liked. "How about dulce de leche cupcakes?"

"'Leche' means 'milk,' right?" Tamiko asked.

I nodded. "'Dulce de leche' basically means 'sweet milk,' and it's like a caramel made with milk cooked down with sugar. You can buy it premade in the store. We make a cinnamon cupcake filled with dulce de leche, and top with a dulce de leche buttercream."

"That sounds *amazing!*" Tamiko said.

"How about we go for a quick shopping trip after lunch to get supplies, and then we can bake after dinner?" her mom suggested.

"Yes!" Tamiko agreed. "Also, we need to get Mia her own bleach pen while we're there."

"Oh boy," Mrs. Sato said. "What are you two up to?"

"Being creative, that's what," Tamiko replied.

"Nothing wild," I assured her mom.

Tamiko grinned. "Speak for yourself."

"I was thinking of maybe a hike at the bird sanctuary," Mr. Sato said. He looked at Dad and Kai. "What do you think? I've got an extra pair of binoculars, Alex."

"I'd like that," Dad said. He glanced at me. "Are you okay with the plan, Mia?"

I nodded. "Have fun!" I told him. Then I took out my phone. "Before we go, I should text Katie for that cupcake recipe."

Katie got right back to me, and I had a shopping list ready on my phone as we headed out to the supermarket. Mrs. Sato already had flour and sugar, so we picked up buttermilk, eggs, cinnamon, butter, and a jar of dulce de leche. In the baking section I found one of those beginner pastry bag kits, with a few assorted plastic tips, and we picked that up, too.

"What color cupcake liners should we get?" Tamiko wondered, looking at the different colors and patterns in the display.

"Well, the frosting is kind of light brown," I told her, "and the dulce de leche is a nice golden brown, so maybe something that would go with that."

Tamiko picked out gold foil cupcake wrappers,

and we even found some tiny, round, edible gold balls that would look pretty on top.

When we got back to the house, Tamiko was practically bouncing up and down with excitement as we unpacked the bags.

"Mom, the AC is on. It's not too hot. We have to bake these cupcakes now, before dinner," Tamiko said.

"Fine with me," Mrs. Sato said, "as long as you don't mind if I hang out and watch. I want to see a cupcake expert at work."

I grinned. "I'm not an expert. But I guess I know something about baking."

When I bake with the Cupcake Club, I do a lot of the decorating. But each of us helps with the baking, and I was surprised how easy it seemed to do now—even without Katie coaching me, like she sometimes did.

"First, we need to measure out the dry ingredients into this bowl," I said, motioning to the medium-size mixing bowl Mrs. Sato had found for us. Tamiko carefully measured the flour, baking powder, baking soda, cinnamon, and salt, and mixed them together.

"Then we put the butter and sugar into this bowl"—I pointed to the bigger bowl—"and use a mixer in it until they're totally light and fluffy."

The Satos didn't have a fancy stand mixer like we normally used, but their hand mixer with the beaters worked just fine. Tamiko and I took turns until the butter-and-sugar mixture was just right. Then we added the eggs, one at a time, and I showed Katie's trick of cracking each one into a measuring cup first. That way you could fish out any shells; or if you got a bad egg, you wouldn't ruin the whole batter.

Next, we added the buttermilk, and then the flour mixture, a little at a time. Some of the flour puffed out and got on our clothes, and we laughed. It's funny. I was usually fussy about not getting flour on my black clothes, but here I didn't mind so much. Maybe Tamiko's easygoing attitude was rubbing off on me.

Finally, we had a nice, smooth batter.

"Here's another trick of Katie's," I said. "Use an ice-cream scoop to put your batter into the cup-cake pan. That way each cupcake will have the same amount of batter."

"This is like watching a cooking show," Mrs. Sato remarked. She'd been sipping on iced coffee as she watched us. "You're very professional, Mia."

"Lots of practice," I told her.

We slid the cupcake pan into the preheated oven, and I set a timer on my phone for twenty minutes.

"This is a good time to clean up the mess we've made so far," I said. "And then, we can make the frosting so it will be ready when the cupcakes are cool."

Tamiko saluted me. "Aye-aye, Captain Cupcake!"

We washed out the bowls and the beaters, and then I measured out more butter, sugar, and some of the dulce de leche to make the frosting. Tamiko used the beaters on the mixture until the frosting was nice and smooth.

"We should keep that in the fridge until we're ready," I suggested. Then my timer beeped, and Mrs. Sato pulled the cupcakes out of the oven for us. I poked the top of one with my finger, and it sprang back.

"You can use a toothpick to make sure the cupcakes are cooked through, but I can tell these are perfect," I explained.

Mrs. Sato put them on a cooling rack, and Tamiko sniffed the air.

"They smell soooooo good!" she said. "I can't wait to eat them!"

"They'll be even better when we're finished,"

I said. "They should be cool enough soon for the filling."

I snipped the corner of a pastry bag and put a tip with a wide circle inside the bag and through the small hole I'd made. Then I filled the bag with dulce de leche.

Tamiko raised her eyebrows. "What sorcery is this?"

"Watch," I said, and picked up a cupcake, poked the tip of the pastry bag into it, and squeezed. "Now it's got dulce de leche filling."

"I need to try this!" Tamiko cried, and took the pastry bag from me. She filled the cupcakes, one by one.

"You're a natural," I told her.

Then I fitted another pastry bag with a narrow rectangular tip, and stuffed that one with our dulce de leche frosting. I demonstrated how to pipe the frosting in smooth swirls.

Tamiko frowned. "That looks hard."

"You can do it," I assured her, handing her the pastry bag.

Tamiko piped the frosting onto a cupcake. It came out in thin ribbons that laid sort of flat on the top of the cupcake.

"See? It's awful!" she said.

"It's not bad," I told her. "Just sprinkle it with the gold balls."

Tamiko did just that. "It's better."

"They don't have to be perfect," I said. "Besides, we can always eat the imperfect ones."

Tamiko waggled her eyebrows. "You mean, before dinner?"

We looked at Mrs. Sato, and she shrugged. "Go ahead. I'm not the cupcake police," she said. "Although it might take a cupcake bribe to keep me from turning you in."

"Let's finish them first," I said, and we took turns frosting them. In the end we had a very pretty plate of twelve cupcakes, decked out in their gold wrappers and decorations.

Mrs. Sato snapped a photo with her camera. "Gorgeous! I'm going to post these!"

"Be sure to give us credit, Ayumi," Tamiko said.

I was a little surprised to hear Tamiko call her mom by her first name, but Mrs. Sato didn't flinch.

"I *always* give credit," her mom replied.

Tamiko turned to me. "Mia, you are such a pro with food. You should come to work with me on Sunday at Molly's Ice-Cream Shop. I'll ask Allie's mom, but I'm sure she won't mind."

"You mean, work behind the counter?" I asked,

remembering the long line out the door. "I've never worked in a shop before."

"It's easy," Tamiko assured me. "I'll make it happen, don't worry, Cupcake!"

She picked up two cupcakes and handed me one. Then she bumped her cupcake against mine, like we were toasting with glasses.

"To cupcakes and ice cream, a perfect pair," she said.

"To friendship," I added, and Tamiko grinned.

We took a bite out of our cupcakes, and I got some of the frosting, filling, and cinnamon cake, all at the same time. It was delicious.

But even nicer was the feeling that came over me that Tamiko was more than just some random daughter of my dad's friends. She was *my* friend. This trip was turning out to have some pretty sweet surprises!

I hoped that helping out at Molly's on Sunday would be sweet too—and not an ice-cream disaster! The last thing I wanted was my new friendship with Tamiko to melt away!

CHAPTER 8

Aaron and I Meet Again!

*T*amiko and I hung out and stayed up late at night, talking and sharing our favorite fashion bloggers on our phones. On Saturday, we both woke up to the sound of people getting ready—a running shower, a whistling teakettle, and lots of talking.

I knew Dad and Tamiko's parents were leaving early to go to the college—there were a bunch of events during the day, before the reunion at night. Kai had a bunch of stuff planned for me and Tamiko, and I was feeling kind of excited to see what the day would bring.

I rummaged through my bag, looking for something to wear. For the first time in weeks, I was kind of regretting my all-black wardrobe. I remembered a blue sundress I had back in my closet at home, and sighed. It would have been perfect for a day like today. But the black shorts and black scoop-neck T-shirt I put on were cute, and I added a silver necklace with a dangling black rose.

Downstairs, the adults and Kai were busy digging into a bag of steaming hot bagels.

"Good morning, girls," Mrs. Sato said. "I know these aren't as good as New York bagels, but they're not bad."

"They smell great," I said, taking a seat and pouring myself a glass of orange juice.

"We're going to be leaving in a few minutes," Dad announced. "Are you sure you'll be okay today?"

"Don't worry, Mr. Cruz," Kai said. "I've texted everyone with today's schedule, so you'll know where we'll be."

Tamiko reached for her phone and checked it out. "We're going to the movies at eleven this morning?" she asked.

"The first matinee of the day is always the cheapest," Kai said. "We're meeting Layla there at ten thirty, so we can get good seats."

"Who's Layla?" I asked.

"It's Kai's gorgeous girlfriend," Tamiko explained, and Kai blushed a little. "Seriously, she could be a model. She's really, really stunning."

"That's not why I like her," Kai said. "She has an even more beautiful personality."

"That's how I feel about my friend Emma," I said. "She's a professional model, but she's also one of the sweetest, nicest people I know."

"You're friends with an actual model?" Tamiko asked. "Of course you are. I bet everyone from New York City knows a model or an actor."

"Well, I only live in the city part-time now," I explained. "I live in New Jersey most of the time. That's where the Cupcake Club is, and Emma's part of the club. It's Katie, Emma, and Alexis."

"Oh, right. A chef, a model, and a female Kai," Tamiko replied. "Maybe I can meet them one day."

She craned her neck toward her mom. "Can we go visit Mia in the fall?"

Mrs. Sato smiled at my dad, and I could tell they were happy we were getting along so well.

"We can talk about it," she said. "I haven't been to the city in ages."

"That might be fun," Mr. Sato agreed.

"Whoot!" Tamiko cheered.

Then her mom changed the subject. "Kai, maybe you can take the girls to the mall for me this afternoon. I was thinking that Mia could help

Tamiko pick out an outfit for the dinner at the Japan Society."

Tamiko groaned and leaned back in her chair. "This again? Can't you please drop it?"

"Tamiko!" her father said sternly. "Please watch your tone with your mother. We can talk more about this later, but the three of us have to get going."

The parents gave us hugs and hurried outside. Kai, Tamiko, and I cleaned up the breakfast dishes.

"We're leaving in a half hour for the movie," Kai announced, and then went upstairs.

Tamiko walked out into her backyard, and I followed her. She sank into a chair.

"I wish Ayumi would stop bugging me about that outfit," she said. "She just doesn't get it."

I nodded. "I kind of get it. My mom's a stylist, so I always feel like she's going to be extra-critical of the clothes I design. Mostly, she's nice about it, though."

Tamiko's eyes widened. "Your mom's a stylist?" she asked. "It's official. You have the coolest life ever."

I didn't know what to say to that. I mean, I could have corrected her, but the more I thought about it, the more I realized my life was pretty cool. I had awesome friends, and a mom with connections in the fashion industry, and I got to spend every other weekend in an exciting city.

"I guess my life is pretty cool," I said. "But yours is too. You live in a beautiful beach town and work at the best ice-cream shop in the world. And you have a great blog."

Tamiko sat up. "Yeah, I guess my life's not so bad," she agreed. "Hey, can you show me some of your mom's stuff? Does she style for magazines and runways and things like that?"

"She used to, but now she mostly works as a personal stylist," I told her, and we looked on my phone at photos of mom's clients until Kai said it was time to go.

The movie theater was a small one near the Bayville boardwalk. When we got there a girl with shiny brown hair walked up to us.

"Hi, Kai. Hi, Tamiko," she said, and then smiled at me. "You must be Mia."

"Also known as Cupcake," said Tamiko, and I figured I was going to be stuck with the nickname.

"And you must be Layla," I said.

"I'm psyched to see this movie," she said. "I'm not usually into superhero movies, but I loved the first one, with that secret mountain of women warriors. Girl power!" Layla cheered loudly.

"Yeah, it was awesome!" Tamiko agreed. "Surprisingly good choice, Kai."

"You're welcome," Kai said. "Come on. Let's get some snacks before we sit down."

After the teenager by the front door scanned our tickets on Kai's phone, we got on the snack line. I looked at the food list, frowning.

"It's kind of early for movie snacks," I said.

"Are you kidding? It's never too early for popcorn," Tamiko said. "We can share."

As I nodded to her, I noticed a boy in a tie-dye T-shirt leaving the counter, carrying a big bucket of popcorn and a drink.

"Aaron!" I called out, and Tamiko raised an eyebrow at me.

Aaron turned around and laughed. "We have to stop meeting like this!"

He walked over to us.

"Aaron, this is Tamiko," I said, introducing them.

"How do you know someone from Bayville?" Tamiko asked me.

"Oh, I'm not from Bayville," Aaron replied. "I'm visiting with my family."

He nodded across the room, where two adults and a little girl were waiting for him.

"My dad and I are staying with Tamiko and her family," I told him.

"Nice shirt," Tamiko remarked to Aaron.

"Thanks," he said. "I just really like tie-dye, I guess."

"Are you going to see *Return to the Mountain*?" I asked him.

Aaron shook his head. "Too scary for Sadie, my sister. We're seeing something with bunnies."

He looked back at his family. "I'd better go. See ya, Mia. Hey, that rhymes!"

I laughed. "I can't think of anything that rhymes with 'Aaron.'"

Aaron grinned and headed off.

"Say hi to Karen, Aaron!" Tamiko called out. Aaron turned around and grinned again.

"Who's Karen?" I asked her.

Tamiko shrugged. "I don't know, but it rhymes." We both giggled.

We ordered popcorn and drinks, and then Tamiko looked at me. "He was cute," she said. "You should get his number. Or add him on SuperSnap."

I felt my cheeks get warm. "It's not like that. He's just some random guy I keep running into."

"Come on. You were both flirting with each other!" Tamiko said. We paid for our snacks and walked away from the counter. "What if you never see him again?"

I thought about that and felt a tiny pang—it had been fun bumping into him again and again.

"He seems nice, but I don't know anything about him," I said. "And besides, what's the point? It's not like we both live in the same town."

Tamiko nodded. "Makes sense, I guess. My friend Sierra would have a bunch to say right now about summer romance, but that's not really my thing."

Kai and Layla were patiently waiting for us over by the wall.

"Come on! The best seats will be gone," Kai urged.

But inside the theater, there were still plenty of seats. Tamiko and I sat pretty much in the middle of the theater.

"The best view is a little higher," Kai said. "Layla and I will be a few rows behind you."

They walked away, and Tamiko and I looked at each other and giggled.

"I guess they want to be alone," I said.

"See? Mom and Dad think Kai is so perfect, volunteering to hang out with us all day, but this was probably some scheme to get Layla to spend time with him," she guessed. "He adores her."

I shrugged. "I don't blame him. Layla seems pretty awesome."

The lights dimmed, and we settled in for the movie. After two hours of women warriors flying on eagles and shooting arrows at bad guys, we streamed back out into the lobby. I looked around, hoping to see the flash of a brightly colored T-shirt, but I didn't see one.

"What's on the schedule next?" Tamiko asked.

"Bowling," Kai said. "Then chilling. Then dinner at Layla's family's restaurant."

"No way!" Tamiko said. "Your family owns a restaurant?"

Layla nodded. "Plantain. It's just a few blocks away from that ice-cream shop where you work."

"I know that place!" Tamiko exclaimed. "It's Dominican food, right? I keep asking Mom and Dad to take us there, but we've never gone."

"I'm glad you're excited," Layla said. "I really think you'll like the food."

I had to give it to Kai—he was really good at planning fun things to do. The bowling alley was decorated in a 1950s retro style with corny but fun old music playing on the speakers, and we got chicken tenders and fries at the snack bar there for lunch. Then we went back at the house for "chill out" time, and Tamiko and I crashed. When we woke up, I got dressed in my skirt that Tamiko had fixed, happy that I had someplace to wear it.

There was a long line outside Plantain when we got there with Kai and Layla, but Layla walked right past it up to the entrance. The woman behind the stand had curly hair like Layla's, pulled black with a red headband. She smiled at us.

"Are these your friends, Layla?" she asked.

"Yes, Aunt Rayna," Layla replied. "This is Kai; and his sister, Tamiko; and their friend Mia."

"We saved a table for you," she said.

"Thanks," Layla replied.

As Layla's aunt led us to our table, Layla told us, "This is weird. I'm so used to working here, not eating here."

"You work here?" Tamiko asked.

Layla nodded. "I wait tables a few nights a week—almost every night during the summer. My father and my uncle do all the cooking."

"I think you should order for us, then," I said.

"Yeah, maybe we can get a few dishes and share them, so we can taste everything," Kai said.

"Sure!" Layla agreed. "Let me go into the kitchen and tell Papá we're here."

About fifteen minutes later we were eating a feast. There were plantains—banana-like vegetables that are starchier and less sweet. Beef stew, and chicken cooked in a tomatoey sauce, and beans and crispy rice that reminded me of my mom's cooking. I took lots of pictures to send to Katie, and Layla's dad came out to meet us while we were eating.

"This is the most delicious food I have ever eaten!" Tamiko burst out when Layla introduced him to us.

"I can't stop eating it," I added.

Layla's dad grinned. "Kai, you can bring your sister and your friend here anytime," he said, and Kai looked relieved and happy at the same time.

"A dad win for Kai," Tamiko whispered to me. "Bringing your sister with you will get you parent points every time."

When we left the restaurant, the sun was setting, and we walked around downtown just like we'd done on our first night. As we approached Molly's, Tamiko ran forward.

"Come on, Cupcake. Let's go see if Allie's there!" she said, and I ran after her, while Kai and Layla hung behind.

The shop was starting to get crowded, but Tamiko and I bypassed the line. Allie was behind the ice-cream counter. She saw us and waved.

"Yo, Alley Cat!" Tamiko called out.

Allie grinned. "Glad you're here. Mom says Mia can help tomorrow, no problem."

"Great," I said, hiding my nervousness.

"And I wanted to show you something," Allie said. She held up a paper ice-cream cup. Inside was what looked like vanilla ice cream with blue swirled into it.

"What do you think?" she asked. "Does it look like waves?"

"It does!" Tamiko replied, and I nodded my head in agreement.

"You know what would be cool?" I asked. "Little gummy fish, swimming in the waves!"

Allie gasped. "Mia, that would be perfect! I wish we had some."

I remembered something. "They sell them at the candy shop that's near here." I turned to Tamiko. "Want to go get some?"

"Sure thing, Cupcake!" she said, and we ran out of the shop, past Kai and Layla, who were sitting on a bench outside.

"We're going to the candy shop and coming right back!" Tamiko yelled at her brother.

I bought a big bag of the gummy fish with my

spending money because I was excited to see how they would look on Allie's ice-cream ocean. When we got back, we handed the bag over to Allie, who carefully placed three fish on the ice cream.

"Adorable!" Allie said.

Tamiko picked up the ice cream, turned to the waiting customers, and held it up.

"Who wants today's brand-new special?" she yelled. "An ocean of vanilla ice cream with blueberry swirl and topped with gummy fish."

"That sounds good," said a woman stepping up to the counter.

"One Friendly Fish special!" Tamiko called out.

Allie laughed. "You're not even supposed to be working, Tamiko," she said. "Do you two want one?"

Tamiko and I looked at each other. We'd eaten a big dinner, but . . .

"Yes, please, Alley Cat," Tamiko said.

Allie made two and handed them to us. "No charge. Thanks for the fish."

"No problem!" I said, and we brought our ice cream outside.

Kai shook his head when he saw us. "How can you eat after that big dinner we had?"

"The question is, how can we *not* eat something

so delicious?"Tamiko asked, dipping her spoon into her cup. "What's next on the schedule."

"What's next is we go home," Kai said. "You're both working tomorrow, right? You should get to sleep early."

Tamiko rolled her eyes. "Yes, *Dad*," she answered, but didn't argue with Kai, and neither did I. It had been a really long, really fun day.

As for tomorrow . . . I wasn't sure what to expect!

CHAPTER 9

Working at Molly's

"Are you sure you're going to be okay? I mean, you won't turn into dust if you wear something that's not black, will you?" Tamiko asked.

I had emerged from Tamiko's room wearing the pink-and-turquoise Molly's Ice Cream T-shirt she had given me, along with my black skinny jeans and a pair of Tamiko's sneakers, which happened to be purple.

"I'll live," I replied. "It's a cute shirt."

"Awesome," Tamiko said. Then she cupped her hands around her mouth. "Ayumi! Can we please get a ride?"

Tamiko's mom came into the kitchen, yawning. Apparently, the parents had all gotten in pretty late last night. Dad had slept even later than I had.

"Sure, Tamiko," she said. "You're going in early?"

"We need to show Mia the ropes," Tamiko explained, and I started to feel nervous again.

"I don't want to mess things up," I said. "I can just hang out here today while you work."

"No way!" Tamiko insisted. "You're gonna be great!"

"Thanks," I said. "At least I look like the rest of you now."

Mrs. Sato drove us back to Molly's, and it felt weird to walk inside the completely empty shop. It was eleven thirty in the morning, and Molly's didn't open until noon. Allie and her mom were there, wiping down the tables.

"Good morning, Alley Cat; good morning Ms. S.," Tamiko greeted them. "I've brought our secret weapon!"

Allie's mom smiled at me. "Thanks for helping out today, Mia. It's been so busy lately, and I hear you know your way around food."

"You should see her bake cupcakes," Tamiko said. "She could be on a cooking show."

"That's why I thought you could help me behind the counter," Allie said. "Sierra runs the register, and Tamiko takes the orders and helps me makes cones and things. But if we get a lot of sundae orders, we get pretty backed up. It can get pretty hectic."

"I'd love to make some sundaes," I said.

Allie motioned for me to follow her behind the counter.

"I don't mind scooping the ice cream—that's tricky, and I've gotten really good at it," she said. "Most sundae orders are custom, like a customer will ask for chocolate sauce and walnuts and whipped cream, and I'll tell you those. Then we have our special sundaes. We're offering the Friendly Fish from yesterday as a sundae, with blueberry sauce and whipped cream on top. And I've been trying to think of another beach-themed sundae we could do."

Tamiko joined us. "Let's come up with something!"

"Maybe you can show me the toppings you have?" I asked. "Oh, and I should find out what flavors you have. Like, do you have any beachy flavors?"

"Tropical Treat—that's mango ice cream with chunks of pineapple in it," Allie replied.

"Mmmm, that sounds delicious," I said.

"It's a good base for a beachy sundae, but we need to beachify it even more," Tamiko said.

Allie's mom walked up, carrying a small plastic

box with a lid. "I bought these from my supplier at the start of summer. Maybe you can figure out what to do with them."

Allie opened the box to reveal a whole bunch of those tiny paper umbrellas in all different colors— the kind they put in drinks in restaurants. Tamiko squealed.

"These are perfect!" she cried. "They look like beach umbrellas. Now we just need something to put on top of the ice cream that looks like sand."

"Graham crackers!" I blurted out, feeling Tamiko's excitement. "Crushed up."

Allie's mom nodded. "I've got some in the kitchen. I use them for the s'mores ice cream."

Allie scooped some of the Tropical Treat ice cream into a cup. Tamiko ran into the kitchen and came back with a box of graham crackers. She crushed them in the cookie crushing station (they had one, Allie explained, for the crushed sandwich cookies they used for the mix-ins). She sprinkled it on top of the ice cream and then stuck in a green umbrella.

"Cute!" Allie announced. "But it needs something."

I looked through the jars of ice-cream toppings and mix-ins. Sprinkles, chocolate chips, cereal bits . . . Everything sounded delicious, and there were some toppings I never would have thought of myself.

"Jelly beans!" I cried. "See how they're kind of curved? They could look like seashells."

"Ooh, yes, and they'd add some color," Tamiko said. She picked up the jar of jelly beans and took out a small scoop. Then she placed a few on top of the cookie/sand.

"Perfecto!" she cried, and then took her phone from her pocket and started taking pictures.

"What's perfecto?" Sierra asked as she walked through the door. "Oh, hi, Mia!"

"Hi, Sierra," I said with a wave. "We just made a beachy sundae."

Sierra looked over the counter. "Cute! You should call it A Day at the Beach!"

Tamiko talked as she typed into her phone. "'Every day is a day at the beach at Molly's. Come on down today for our sundae special: Tropical Treat ice-cream topic with a graham cracker cookie crumble and fruity jelly beans. Or get your blue-berry on with our Friendly Fish sundae featuring syrup made from local wild blueberries.'"

"Great job, girls!" Ms. S. said. She looked at the clock. "I'm off to the kitchen. Time to open the doors. Give a yell if you get swamped."

She walked away, and Tamiko ran around the corner and over to the chalkboard. She wrote the sundae names on the board. Sierra made her way to the cash register and pressed some buttons to turn it on. Allie handed me a pair of clear, plastic gloves.

"Please put these on," she said. "If we get any sundae orders, I'll give them to you and tell you what toppings to add."

"Got it!" I said, and took a deep breath.

Ting-a-ling. The bell on the front door jingled as the first customers walked in—a grandparent-looking older couple.

"Two cups of vanilla, please," the woman told Tamiko.

"Vanilla is delicious, but wouldn't you love our Friendly Fish sundae instead?" Tamiko asked. "That's vanilla swirled with blueberry syrup, and topped with gummy fish."

"That sounds nice, but I'm afraid the gummy fish would stick to our teeth," the woman replied.

"Vanilla it is!" Tamiko said, and Allie quickly went to work scooping out the ice cream into cups.

"Can I give you both a sprinkle of happy, Rose?" Allie asked them.

"Yes, we always look forward to those," the woman replied.

Allie spooned rainbow sprinkles over both cups. "Here's your sprinkle of happy!" She handed over the two cups of ice cream with a huge grin.

"Does Tamiko always try to sell the sundaes like that?" I asked Allie.

Tamiko heard me. "You bet I do. Sell, sell, sell!"

I laughed. "We could use you when we sell cupcakes at the street fair next week."

"You don't need me, you just need *confidence*, Cupcake!" Tamiko told me, and I knew she was right. I'd always thought I was confident, but I was practically shy next to Tamiko.

The next customers just wanted ice-cream cones, and after that came a mom with toddlers who wanted kiddie cups, so I wasn't busy at first. But when the next customer came in, I was up.

Allie handed me a cup filled with ice cream. "This one gets chocolate sauce, strawberries, and bananas," she said. I carefully spooned the sauce, then the strawberries, and then arranged banana slices in a neat circle around the rim of the cup. I gave it back to Allie.

"Beautiful!" she said. "But when it gets busy, you don't have to worry about making it perfect.

You can put the bananas on any old way."

"Sloppy bananas!" Tamiko yelled, and Allie shook her head and finished off the cup with rainbow sprinkles. "And here is your sprinkle of happy!"

Things started to pick up quickly. Allie would slide a cup of ice cream in front of me and tell me what to put on it. There were so many toppings, but they were neatly organized. Most people just wanted chocolate sauce and whipped cream, so it was easy to do. And thanks to Tamiko, we sold a lot of Friendly Fish and A Day at the Beach specials, and those weren't complicated at all.

About an hour in I was busy putting jelly beans on a beach sundae when I heard a familiar voice.

"Mia! Do you work here?"

I looked up to see Aaron, waiting on line for ice cream. I was surprised to see him, but also surprised to see him wearing a black T-shirt.

"I'm just helping out," I told him. "Nice shirt."

He grinned. "I like yours, too."

Then Allie handed me another cup, and I had to stop talking to him. She leaned toward me. "Who is he?"

"Just some guy I keep bumping into," I told her. "I mean, he's nice, though."

There were a few more orders to do before Aaron got to the counter and placed his order for a Friendly Fish sundae. I made it for him, and then Allie nodded at me.

"Why don't you finish it?" she asked.

I walked up to the counter and spooned the rainbow sprinkles on top of the sundae. "Here's your sprinkle of happy," I said.

"Thanks," Aaron replied. "So, how long are you here for?"

"We're leaving tomorrow," I said, and felt a little pang as I said it. I didn't want to leave! "How about you?"

"We leave on Wednesday," he said. "Maybe, um, I'll see you before you go?"

"Maybe," I said, and my heart started to beat fast. Was he going to ask for my number? Add me on SuperSnap? But he just moved down the line and paid Sienna.

After he left, Tamiko looked back at me. "You should have gotten the deets!" she said.

I laughed. "Sorry, can't talk. Gotta make this fudge sundae."

The rest of the afternoon flew by! I couldn't believe it when the college students who worked at the shop came to take over our shift. Ms. S. came out and thanked me for helping. Then she slipped me an envelope.

"This is for your work today, Mia," she said. "Thank you."

Then Sierra gave slipped some cash into my hand. "And here's your share of the tips."

"You didn't have to do that," I told them. "I just wanted to help, and it was fun."

I looked at Tamiko, Allie, and Sierra, and I knew that if I already didn't have the Cupcake Club, I would be right at home with these Sundae Sisters.

"What are your plans for your last night in Bayville?" Ms. S. asked.

"I'm not sure," I said, and turned to Tamiko. "Did Kai schedule something?"

"Yes, but we are *not* playing mini golf," she said, with a gleam in her eye. "I've got something special planned for us."

I grinned. I had always wanted to play mini golf, but now that I knew Tamiko, I couldn't wait to see what she had in store.

CHAPTER 10

I Model for *Tamiko's Take*!

Okay, so I'm going to call this blog post 'City Chic in a Small Town,'" Tamiko announced.

We were in her room, with all my clothes (the ones that were still clean, anyway) spread out on her bed.

"Are you sure you want me to model for your blog?" I asked. "I'm a designer, not a model."

"You're fabulous, and you know it," Tamiko shot back. "The thing is, your clothes definitely are chic. But maybe, you know, we can add some color. If you aren't against that."

I looked down at my colorful Molly's T-shirt. "I think I'm ready to add a little more color to my wardrobe," I told her.

She threw open her closet, and I started to feel excitement. Tamiko's clothes were awesome, and I was going to get to try some on!

She pulled out a blue plaid skirt. "How about this skirt, with your black tank top?"

"The shoes have to be just right, though," I said. I held up some black sneakers. "Maybe these?"

"Adorbs!" Tamiko replied. "With your hair in a tight ponytail or bun, and maybe some dangling earrings. Do you wear earrings?"

I pulled back my hair to show her my black sparkly studs.

"Excellent!" she said. "That's one outfit down. Now we need about three more."

I picked up a short-sleeved, knee-length black jersey dress. "Could we do something with this? What about the denim vest you just made."

"That's so genius!" Tamiko cried, and we paired that with white sneakers and a red choker necklace.

Tamiko picked up a gauzy black top I had. "This might look nice with my leggings," she said, and pulled a pair of red leggings with tiny white polka dots on them.

"Those might work with the shirt, and my black flats," I said, and then remembered something. "Are these the leggings your mom doesn't want you to wear to that dinner?"

Tamiko nodded. "Yeah, can you believe that? Just because all her friends are there, and she says I'll make her look like a bad parent."

"Is it a fancy dinner?" I asked.

"Well, yeah, but I'm not going to wear some dumb prom dress just to sit at a table and listen to boring speeches," she replied. Then she changed the topic. "Ooh, I've got a headband that will go great with this!"

We picked out two more outfits, and then Tamiko took me outside for the photo shoot. First, we took some shots on the front steps.

"Hold on to the railing with your left hand. Yes, perfect!" she instructed me.

Mrs. Sato stuck her head out the front door. "Tamiko, it's almost time for dinner."

"We're working against the sunlight, Ayumi!" Tamiko replied, and her mom just shook her head and closed the door.

"Should we finish up later?" I asked Tamiko.

"Nah, it'll be fine," she assured me, and I ran inside to change my clothes for the next shoot.

Tamiko had me pose on a lounge chair in her backyard, leaning against a bicycle, and sitting under a tree on a picnic blanket. I just followed her instructions and had no idea if I was doing a good job or not—but I knew the clothes were on point, so I wasn't too worried.

Everybody was already eating at the table by the time we were finished, but nobody seemed to mind that we were late. Tamiko and I dug into some teriyaki salmon with rice and pickled vegetables, and I ate every bite on my plate.

"Mia, we need to hit the road by ten tomorrow," Dad said. "That should give you plenty of time to wake up and get packed. And I'd love to take everyone out for breakfast before we go."

"Uncle Billy's Pancakes!" Tamiko said. "That place is the best."

"Sounds good," Dad replied.

"You really don't need to do that," Mr. Sato said.

"It will be a nice way to say good-bye," Dad responded. "Plus, we can't thank you enough for letting us stay with you. It's been such a good time."

"It's been awesome," I chimed in. "Thank you all so much."

Mrs. Sato smiled warmly. "You two are the best houseguests anyone could ask for."

"Yeah, way better than Dad's other college

friend, Desmond," Tamiko remarked. "He snored so loud he shook the house!"

"She's not lying," Tamiko's mom said. "So, after dinner, who wants to watch a movie?"

"That would be nice," I said. "But I need to do something with Tamiko first. Is that okay?"

"Of course," she replied, and Tamiko looked at me with raised eyebrows.

"Should I know about this?" Tamiko asked.

I shook my head. "No," I replied. "It's just an idea that I had."

After we finished eating and helped clean up, Tamiko and I went back up to her room. I took my crocheted black top from my bag.

"You want to do another shoot?" she asked.

I shook my head. "No, this is for you," I told her. "You have that black skirt with the little silver stars on it that would look so pretty with this. For your dinner."

"Wait a second, I—" She stopped herself. "They would look cute together. And it's not a boring outfit. And I think Mom might like it."

"I think your mom would love it," I said. "With some cute sandals?"

"And a silver headband! And star earrings!" Tamiko added.

"Try it on!" I said, and went into my little room to give her some privacy. I took out my phone.

I miss you soooo much! I typed to Katie. Can't wait to see you! Home Tuesday.

Katie wrote to me. Hurry home!

I sent her a bunch of frowny-face emojis. I felt so weird. I didn't want to leave Bayville, but I missed home so much at the same time!

"Ta-da!" Mia burst into the room in the black-and-silver outfit. She looked amazing.

I clapped my hands together. "You are perfect! Let's go show your mom."

We walked down the stairs, with Tamiko doing a slow, model descent. Her mom stopped in her tracks when she saw Tamiko.

"You look great, Tamiko. Are you doing a photo shoot?"

Tamiko shook her head. "No, this is what I'm wearing to the Japan Society dinner. Mia gave me the shirt."

Mrs. Sato hugged me. "Mia, are you sure you don't want to move in?"

I laughed. "I'm not sure if my mom would like that."

"You'd better get to sleep on the early side, *mija*," Dad said.

"Okay," I said, but of course Tamiko and I stayed up really late that night, talking. We woke up at nine, and even though I was tired, I tried to act like I wasn't, so I wouldn't get a lecture from Dad.

We ate breakfast at Uncle Billy's Pancakes, and I got chocolate-chip pancakes and sausages, and I ate them extra slowly because I didn't want the morning to end. But it did, and I couldn't hold back my tears as we all hugged good-bye in the parking lot.

"I'll miss you, Cupcake," Tamiko said.

"I'll miss you, too, Ice Cream," I told her, and she grinned.

Then Dad and I got into our car and made our way home. We drove through the downtown area again, on the way back to the highway. When we passed the T-shirt shop, I asked Dad if we could stop.

"Can I just go in really fast?" I asked him. "I won't be long. There's something I need to get."

Dad pulled into a space right in front of the spot. "Take your time."

I went inside and headed for the rack of tie-dyed T-shirts with their bright, swirling colors. I found one with pretty shades of blue, purple, and pink and bought it with my Molly's money.

A tiny part of me did it to remember the cute

boy in the tie-dyed shirt. But a bigger part of me did it because I didn't feel like wearing all black anymore. Thanks to Tamiko and this cute beach town, my dark mood and meh was gone.

"Can I wear this outside?" I asked the salesclerk, and she showed me where the dressing room was. When I came back to the car, Dad raised an eyebrow.

"Now that's colorful," he said.

"Yes, it is," I replied, and we headed on the road again.

I checked my phone, which was blowing up with a group text between my friends.

Alexis had begun the chat. We still don't have a cupcake plan for the street festival!

Let's meet when Mia gets back, Katie suggested.

But don't we need to shop soon? Emma asked.

I grinned. I have some amazing ideas. Hang on.

As we drove north, toward home, I sent my ideas and photo references to Katie, Emma, and Alexis. If we could pull these cupcakes off, the festival was going to be amazing!

CHAPTER 11

I Find My Confidence

All right, Katie, Emma, Mia, Alexis, smile and say 'Cupcake!'"

"Cupcake!"

My friends and I stood in front of our booth at the Maple Grove Summer Street Festival while Katie's stepsister took our photo. After a few shots she handed the phone back to me.

"Thanks, Emily," I said. "I'm going to take some more photos of our display and get them up on our SuperSnap page."

"That's a great idea," Alexis said. "Once people see our booth, they'll have to come get our cupcakes."

"Yeah, we really outdid ourselves," Katie said.

She was right. Our "booth" was a folding table

under a tent, set up on Maple Grove's Main Street. Thanks to my Bayville inspiration, we'd gone with a beach theme. There was a blue tablecloth on the table, with cardboard fish we'd made pinned to the cloth. Paper seagulls hung down from the top of the tent, flying around our heads.

Our cupcakes were beach themed. First, we'd made vanilla cupcakes, with frosting that had rainbow colors swirled in to look like tie-dye—a simple flavor to appeal to a lot of people, but with a colorful look.

Our second cupcake was even more impressive. I'd searched online and found out that you could actually bake cupcake batter into ice-cream cones—the ones with the flat bottoms. We'd made two kinds of batter—chocolate and strawberry. The chocolate cones had chocolate frosting on top that looked just like ice cream, with a candied cherry and sprinkles on top. The strawberry cones had strawberry buttercream along with the cherry and sprinkles. They looked just like ice-cream cones, but they were cupcakes!

The festival officially opened at ten in the morning, and the four of us and Emily stood behind our display, waiting for the customers to arrive. A delicious smell hit our noses.

"That smells like. . . doughnuts!" Katie cried. "Are they frying doughnuts on the spot? We're doomed!"

She ran off to find the doughnut booth, and came back five minutes later with a white paper bag with grease stains on the bottom.

"Freshly made cinnamon-sugar mini doughnuts," she said, handing one to each of us. "They're so delicious! Nobody will buy our cupcakes."

"Oh, they're soooo good!" Emma agreed.

People were starting to stroll down the street, browsing the booths. Something Tamiko had told me came back to me.

You just need confidence, *Cupcake!*

I took a deep breath and channeled my inner Tamiko.

"Get your cupcakes here!" I yelled. "We have Ice-Cream Cone Cupcakes! You won't find them anywhere else!"

Katie looked at me, impressed. "Mia, I've never heard you be so . . . loud!"

I shrugged. "We want customers, don't we?"

She nodded and ran in front of the booth, yelling even louder than I had. "We have Ice-Cream Cone Cupcakes! Get your Ice-Cream Cone Cupcakes here!"

It worked. People started to wander over to our booth.

"What exactly is an Ice-Cream Cone Cupcake?" a woman asked us. She had a little girl with her.

"It's a cupcake baked inside a cone," I said, motioning to the cupcakes. "We have strawberry or chocolate."

"That is so fun!" the woman said. "And easy to eat, too. I'll take a strawberry."

She looked down at the girl. "Do you want an Ice-Cream Cone Cupcake?"

The girl pointed at the tie-dye cupcakes. "I want a pretty cupcake," she said.

The woman nodded. "Okay, we'll take one of those, too."

Emma handed them their cupcakes, Alexis took their money, and when they walked away, we all high-fived.

"Our first sale!" Alexis cried, but we had no time to celebrate because more customers walked up to the booth.

Within about thirty minutes we had a line. People noticed other people walking around with the Ice-Cream Cone Cupcakes, and everybody wanted one. Katie and I didn't have to yell in front of the booth anymore. We got behind the table with Emma and Alexis and sold cupcakes as fast as we could.

"I'll have a tie-dye cupcake, please," I heard as I was counting out change to a customer. And then, "Mia? What are you doing here?"

I looked up to see . . . Aaron! I couldn't believe my eyes.

"Okay, this is weird," I said. "How did you know I was here?"

"I didn't," he replied. "I live in Stonebrook."

Stonebrook is the town right next to Maple Grove. My jaw dropped.

"I live here—in Maple Grove," I said.

Katie nudged me. "Who's your friend?" she asked, eyeing Aaron.

"Remember the boy I met in Bayville? The one I told you about?" I asked. "Well, this is him, Aaron. Aaron, these are my friends—Katie, Alexis, and Emma."

He smiled. "Hi."

I took my phone from my pocket. "I have to send a photo to Tamiko. She's not going to believe this."

"Sure," Aaron said, and I stood next to him and got a selfie of both of us. Then I sent it to Tamiko.

Ice Cream, look who lives in the next town!

She replied right away. OMG, Cupcake, GET THE DEETS, OR I WILL NEVER SPEAK TO YOU AGAIN!

"So, um, can I send this photo to your SuperSnap?" I asked Aaron.

"Sure, I'll add you," Aaron said, taking out his phone.

We added each other on the app.

"Um, so, it was good seeing you again," I said.

"Yeah," he agreed. "So, can I get my cupcake?"

I blushed. "Yes, of course!" I said, and handed him one.

He looked at the tie-dye design and smiled. I wanted to talk more to him, but the booth was so busy that he paid for the cupcake and then waved and walked away.

My friends started talking at once.

"He's cute," Alexis said.

"I think the fact that he lives in Stonebrook is, like, fate," Emma said seriously. "You're probably soul mates."

"I'm not so sure about that," I said. "But seeing him was definitely a nice surprise."

The last few weeks had been full of sweet surprises—like becoming friends with Tamiko, meeting Aaron, swimming in the ocean, and working in an ice-cream shop. I smiled to myself. Was it just a few short weeks ago when the only color I wanted to wear was black? The sweetest surprise of all was remembering that even when I was feeling meh, life was still full of beautiful colors.

Here's a small taste
of the very first book in the

series written by Coco Simon:

SUNDAY SUNDAES

PLOT TWIST

A hot August wind lifted my brown hair and cooled the back of my neck as I waited for the bus to take me to my new school. I hoped I was standing in the right spot. I hoped I was wearing the right thing. I wished I were anywhere else.

My toes curled in my new shoes as I reached into my messenger bag and ran my thumb along the worn spine of my favorite book. I'd packed *Anne of Green Gables* as a good-luck charm for my first day at my new school. The heroine, Anne Shirley, had always cracked me up and given me courage. To me, having a book around was like having an old friend for company. And, boy, did I need a friend right about now.

Ten days before, I'd returned from summer camp

to find my home life completely rearranged. It hadn't been obvious at first, which was almost worse. The changes had come out in drips, and then all at once, leaving me standing in a puddle in the end.

My mom and dad picked me up after seven glorious weeks of camp up north, where the temperature is cool and the air is sweet and fresh. I was excited to get home, but as soon as I arrived, I missed camp. Camp was fun, and freedom, and not really worrying about anything. There was no homework, no parents, and no little brothers changing the ringtone on your phone so that it plays only fart noises. At camp this year I swam the mile for the first time, and all my camp besties were there. My parents wrote often: cheerful e-mails, mostly about my eight-year-old brother, Tanner, and the funny things he was doing. When they visited on Parents' Weekend, I was never really alone with them, so the conversation was light and breezy, just like the weather.

The ride home was normal at first, but I noticed my parents exchanging glances a couple of times, almost like they were nervous. They looked different too. My dad seemed more muscular and was tan, and my mom had let her hair—dark brown and wavy, like mine—grow longer, and it made her look younger. The minute I got home, I grabbed my sweet cat, Diana (named after Anne Shirley's best friend, naturally), and scrambled into my room. Sharing a bunkhouse with eleven other girls for a summer was great, but I was really glad to be back in my own quiet room. I texted SHE'S BAAAACK! to my best friends, Tamiko Sato and Sierra Perez, and then took a really long, hot shower.

It wasn't until dinnertime that things officially got weird.

"You must've really missed me," I said as I sat down at the kitchen table. They'd made all of my favorites: meat lasagna, garlic bread, and green salad with Italian dressing and cracked pepper. It was the meal we always had the night before I left for camp and the night I got back. My mouth started watering.

I grinned as I put my napkin onto my lap.

"We *did* miss you, Allie!" said my mom brightly.

"They talked about you all the time," said Tanner, rolling his eyes and talking with his mouth full of garlic bread, his dinner napkin still sitting prominently on the table.

"Napkin on lapkin!" I scolded him.

"Boys don't use napkins. That's what sleeves are

for," said Tanner, smearing his buttery chin across the shoulder of his T-shirt.

"Gross!" Coming out of the all-girl bubble of camp, I had forgotten the rougher parts of the boy world. I looked to my parents to reprimand him, but they both seemed lost in thought. "Mom? Dad? Hello? Are you okay with this?" I asked, looking to both of them for backup.

"Hmm? Oh, Tanner, don't be disgusting. Use a napkin," said my mom, but without much feeling behind it.

He smirked at me, and when she looked away, he quickly wiped his chin on his sleeve again. It was like all the rules had flown out the window since I'd been gone!

My dad cleared his throat in the way he usually did when he was nervous, like when he had to practice for a big sales presentation. I looked up at him; he was looking at my mom with his eyebrows raised. His dark brown eyes—identical to mine—were *definitely* nervous.

"What's up?" I asked, the hair on my neck prickling a little. When there's tension around, or sadness, I can always feel it. It's not like I'm psychic or anything.

I can just feel people's feelings coming off them in waves. Maybe my parents' fighting as I was growing up had made me sensitive to stuff, or maybe it was from reading so many books and feeling the characters' feelings along with them. Whatever it was, my mom said I had a lot of empathy. And right now my empathy meter was registering *high alert*.

My mom swallowed hard and put on a sunny smile that was a little too bright. Now I was really suspicious. I glanced at Tanner, but he was busy dragging a slab of garlic bread through the sauce from his second helping of lasagna.

"Allie, there's something Dad and I would like to tell you. We've made some new plans, and we're pretty excited about them."

I looked back and forth between the two of them. What she was saying didn't match up with the anxious expressions on their faces.

"They're getting divorced," said Tanner through a mouthful of lasagna and bread.

"What?" I said, shocked, but also . . . kind of not. I felt a huge sinking in my stomach, and tears pricked my eyes. I knew there had been more fighting than usual before I'd left for camp, but I hadn't really seen

this coming. Or maybe I had; it was like divorce had been there for a while, just slightly to the side of everything, riding shotgun all along. Automatically my brain raced through the list of book characters whose parents were divorced: Mia in the Cupcake Diaries, Leigh Botts in *Dear Mr. Henshaw*, Karen Newman in *It's Not the End of the World*. . . .

My mother sighed in exasperation at Tanner.

"Wait, Tanner knew this whole time and I didn't?" I asked.

"Sweetheart," said my dad, looking at me kindly. "This has been happening this summer, and since Tanner was home with us, he found out about it first." Tanner smirked at me, but Dad gave him a look. "I know this is hard, but it's actually really happy news for me and your mom. We love each other very much and will stay close as a family."

"We're just tired of all the arguing. And we're sure you two are too. We feel that if we live apart, we'll be happier. All of us."

My mind raced with questions, but all that came out was, "What about me and Tanner? And Diana? Where are we going to live?"

"Well, I found a great apartment right next to the

playground," said my dad, suddenly looking happy for real. "You know that new converted factory building over in Maple Grove, with the rooftop pool that we always talk about when we pass by?"

"And I've found a really great little vintage house in Bayville. And you won't believe it, but it's right near the beach!"

I stared at them.

Mom swallowed hard and kept talking. "It's just been totally redone, and the room that will be yours has built-in bookcases all around it and a window seat," she said.

"And it has a hot tub," added my dad.

"Right," laughed my mom. "And there are plant-ings in the flower beds around the house, so we can have fresh flowers all spring, summer, and fall!" My mom loved flowers, but my dad grew up doing so much yard work for his parents that he refused to ever let her plant anything here. The house did sound nice, but then something occurred to me.

"Wait, Bayville and Maple Grove? So what about school?" Bayville was ten minutes away!

"Well." My parents shared a pleased look as my mom spoke. "Since my new house is in Bayville, you qualify for seventh grade at the Vista Green School! It's the top-rated school in the district, and it's gorgeous! Everything was newly built just last year. Tan will go to MacBride Elementary."

"Isn't that great?" said my dad.

"Um, *what*? We're changing *schools*?" The lasagna was growing cold on my plate, but how could I eat? I looked at Tanner to see how he was reacting to all this news, but he was nearly finished with his second helping of lasagna and showed no sign of stopping. The shoulder of his T-shirt now had red sauce stains smeared across it. I looked back at my mom.

"Yes, sweetheart. I know it will be a big transition at first. Everything is going to be new for us all! A fresh start!" said my mom enthusiastically.

Divorce. Moving. A new school.

"Is there any *more* news?" I asked, picking at a crispy corner of my garlic bread.

"Actually," my mom began, looking to my dad, "I have some really great news. Dad and I decided it probably wasn't a good idea for me to go on being the chief financial officer of his company. So I've rented a space in our new neighborhood, and . . . I'm opening an ice cream store, just like I've always dreamed!

Ta-da!" She threw her arms wide and grinned.

My jaw dropped as I lifted my head in surprise. "Really?" My mom made the best—I mean the absolute *best*—homemade ice cream in the world. She made a really thick, creamy ice cream base, and then she was willing to throw in anything for flavor: lemon and blueberries, crumbled coffee cake, crushed candy canes, you name it. She was known for her ice cream. I mean, people came to our house and actually asked if she had any in the freezer.

My mom was nodding vigorously, the smile huge on her face. She looked happier and younger than I'd seen her in years. And my dad looked happier than he had in a long time.

"And you two can be the taste testers!" said my mom.

"Yessss!" said Tanner, pumping his fist out and back against his chest. "And our friends, too?" he asked.

"Yes. All of your friends can test flavors too," said my mom.

"Okay, wait." I couldn't take this all in at once. It felt like someone had removed my life and replaced it with a completely new version.

Who were these people? What was my family? *Who was I?*

"Eat your dinner, honey," urged my dad. "It's your favorite. There's plenty of time to talk through all of this."

My eyes suddenly brimmed with tears; I just couldn't help it. Even if—and this was a big "if" for me—this would be a good move for our family, there was still a new house and a new *school*. What about my friends? What about Book Fest, the reading celebration at my school that I helped organize and was set to run this year?

I wiped my eyes with my sleeve. "What about Book Fest?" I said meekly.

My mom stood and came around to hug me. "Oh, Allie, I'm sure they'll still let you come."

I pulled away. "Come? I *run* it! Who's going to run it now? And what will I do instead?"

I scraped my chair away from the table, pulled away from my mom, and raced to my room. Diana was curled up on my bed, and she jumped when I closed the door hard behind me. (It wasn't a slam, but almost.) I grabbed Diana, flopped onto the bed, and had a good cry. Certainly Anne Shirley would have thrown herself onto her bed and cried, at least at first. But what would Hermione Granger have done? Violet Baudelaire? Katniss Everdeen? My favorite characters encountered a lot of troubles, but they usually got through them okay, and it wasn't by lying around crying about them. I sniffed and reached for a tissue, and slid up against my headboard into a sitting position so that I could have a good think, like a plot analysis.

My parents had been unhappy for a long time. I kind of knew that. I mean, I guess we were all unhappy because Mom and Dad fought a lot.

They both worked hard at their jobs, and I knew they were tired, so I always thought a lot of it was just crankiness. Plus Mom was the business manager and my dad ran the marketing group at their company, so I figured since they worked together all day, they just got on each other's nerves after work. But if I really thought about it, I realized that they were like that on the weekends, and even on holidays and vacations. They snapped at each other. They rolled their eyes. And sometimes one of them stomped out of the room. And the more I thought about it, I realized they hadn't spent a lot of time together over the past year. Either Mom would be taking me to soccer and Dad would be staying home with Tanner, or Dad would be doing carpool and errands while Mom went with Tanner to his music lessons. We always ate dinner together, but starting last winter and right up to when I'd left for camp, there had been a lot of pretty quiet meals, with each of us lost in our own thoughts. Mom would talk to me or to Tanner, and Dad would always ask about our days, but they never actually spoke to each other.

I squeezed my eyes shut and tried to think of the last time we'd all been happy together. The night before I left for camp, maybe? We had my favorite dinner, and Dad was teasing that it would be the last great meal before I ate camp food for the summer. Mom joked that we should sneak some lasagna into my shoes, which Tanner thought was a really good idea. Dad ran and picked up one of my sneakers, and Mom pretended to spoon some in. We were being silly and laughing, and I felt warm and snug and cozy. I loved camp and couldn't wait to go every year, but I remembered thinking right then that I'd miss being at the table with my family around me.

Later that night, though, I heard Mom and Dad

fighting about something in their room, like they seemed to do almost every night. Then for seven weeks I went to sleep hearing crickets and giggles instead of angry whispers, along with a few warnings of "Girls, it's time to go to bed!" from my counselors.

Now I heard whispers from Mom and Dad on the other side of the door. They weren't angry, but they didn't sound happy, either. Then I heard the whispers fade as they went downstairs.

I guess I fell asleep, because when I woke up, Dad was sitting on my bed and Mom was standing next to him, looking worried. The lights were out, but my room was bright from the moon.

"Allie," Dad said gently. "You need to brush your teeth and get ready for bed."

"Do you want to talk about anything?" Mom asked as I sat up.

Suddenly I was really annoyed. "Oh, you mean like how you decided to get a divorce and not tell me? Or sell our house and not tell me? Or that I would need to move schools and totally start over again? Nope, nothing to discuss at all." I crossed my arms over my chest.

"Allie," Mom said, and her voice broke. I could

tell she was upset, but I didn't care. "We are divorcing because we think it will make us happier. All of us."

"Speak for yourself," I said. I knew I was being mean, and on any usual day one of them would tell me to watch my tone.

"It is going to be hard," said Dad slowly. "It's going to be an adjustment, and it's going to take a lot of patience from all of us. We are not sugarcoating that part. But it's going to be better. You and Tanner mean everything to us, and Mom and I are going to do what will make you happiest. This separation will make us stronger as a family. Things will be better, and we need you to believe that."

"And what if I don't?" I said. I knew I was on thin ice. Even I could tell that I sounded a little bratty. "What will make me happiest is to stay in this house and go to the same school with my friends and . . ." I thought about it for a second. "Wait, if I'm moving to Bayville, when will I ever see Dad?"

"A lot still needs to be worked out," said Mom. "For now you and Tanner and Diana will live with me at the house in Bayville during the week. Dad will come over every Wednesday, and every other weekend you'll be at Dad's apartment in Maple Grove."

I looked at Dad. "So every other week I'll only see you on Wednesdays?" I felt my eyes filling with tears again.

"We can work things out, Allie," said Dad quickly. "I am still here and I am still your dad and I will always be around."

"I promise you, Allie, we're going to do everything we can to make this better for all of us," Mom said. I couldn't see her face clearly, but I could see that she was trying hard not to cry.

Dad reached over and gave Mom's arm a little squeeze. I sat there looking at them, not being able to remember the last time I'd seen Mom give Dad a kiss hello, or Dad hug Mom. Now here they were, but even that didn't seem right.

"I'm not brushing my teeth," I said. I don't really know why I said that. I guess I just wanted to feel like I was still in control of something, anything. Then I turned away from them and pulled up the covers. All I wanted to do was go to sleep, because I was really hoping I would wake up and this would all be a bad dream.

I woke up and blinked a few times, remembering that I was back in my room at home and not still at camp. Well, home for now.

I slowly got up and listened at the door. I could hear Mom talking and the *clink* of a spoon in a bowl, which meant Tanner was slurping his cereal. I didn't want to stay in my room, but I didn't want to go downstairs either. I grabbed my phone. With all of the drama the night before, I had completely forgotten to check it. I looked at the screen, and there were eighteen messages, ranging from did a big scary monster eat you???? to OMG she came back and now she's gone again! from my best friends, Tamiko and Sierra. I sent a couple of quick texts to them, and within seconds my phone was buzzing, as I'd known it would be.

Just then Mom knocked at my door and opened it. "Good morning, sweetie!" she said with her new Sally Sunshine voice that I was already not liking. "I'm so glad to have my girl home!"

I looked at her. Was she just going to pretend nothing had happened?

Mom came in and sat down on my bed. "Dad

left for work, but I took this week off. The movers are coming in a couple of days, and we'll need time to settle into our new house." She looked at me. I stared at the wall. The wall of my room, where I had lived since I was a baby. I looked at the spot behind the door, and Mom followed my eyes. She sighed. Since I had been tiny, Dad had measured me on the wall on my birthday and had made a little mark at the top of my head. He'd even done it last year, even though I'd told him I was way too old. "I'm going to miss this house," she said softly. "It has a lot of memories."

It was quiet for a second. Mom looked like she was far away.

"You took your first steps in the kitchen," she said, really smiling this time. "And remember your seventh birthday party that we had in the backyard?" I did. It was a fairy tea party, and each kid got fairy wings and a magic wand. There had been so many birthdays and holidays in this house.

I had never lived in another house. All I knew was this one. I knew that there were thirty-eight steps between the front porch and the bus stop. I could run up the stairs to the second floor in eight seconds

(Tanner and I had timed each other), and I knew that the cabinet door in the kitchen where we kept the cookies creaked when you opened it.

"I think you'll like the new house," said Mom. "Houses. You'll have two homes."

I looked straight ahead.

"Your new room has bookcases all around it. I thought of you when I saw it and knew you would love it." Mom looked at me. "And there's a really great backyard to hang out in. I'm thinking about getting a hammock maybe, and definitely some comfy rocking chairs."

"What about my new other house?" I asked.

"Well," Mom said, "Dad's house is an apartment, actually, and it has really cool views. It's modern, and my house is more old-fashioned. It's the best of both worlds!"

I sighed.

Mom sighed. "Honey, I know this is tough."

I still didn't answer. Mom stood up.

"Well, kiddo, we have a lot to do. I'm guessing Tamiko and Sierra are coming over soon?"

I looked at my phone lighting up. "Maybe," I said.

Mom nodded. "Okay. Well, let me know what

you want to do today. It's your first day back. Tomorrow, though, we do need to pack up your room. Dad and I have been packing things up for the past few weeks, but there's still a lot to do."

I looked into the hall. I must have missed the fact that there were some boxes stacked there. One was marked "Mom" and one was marked "Dad."

Mom followed my gaze. "We're trying to make sure there are familiar things in each house. You can split up your room or . . . I was thinking maybe you'd like to get a new bedroom set?" There was that fake bright happy voice again.

I looked around the room. I liked my room. If the house couldn't stay the same, at least my room could. "No," I said. "I want this stuff."

"We should also talk about your new school," Mom said.

I looked down at my feet. My toenails were painted in my camp colors, blue and yellow. I wiggled them.

"You're already enrolled, but I talked to the principal about having you come over to take a tour and maybe meet some of your new teachers."

I shrugged.

"I think it might be good to take a ride over, just

so you are familiar with it before your first day," she said. "It's a bigger school, so you could get the lay of the land. And I've been asking around the new neighborhood, and there are a few girls who will be in your grade."

I nodded.

"Okay," she said brightly. "Well, we have this week to do that, so we'll just find a good time to go."

I swallowed hard.

Mom stood in the doorway and waited a minute, then stepped back into the room quickly, gathered me up in her arms, and hugged me tightly. "It's going to be better, baby girl," she said, kissing the top of my head like she used to when I was little. She was using her normal voice again. "I promise you, it might be hard, but it's definitely going to be better."

I tried really, really hard not to cry. A few tears spilled out, and Mom wiped them away. She took my face in her hands and looked at me. "Now," she said, "first things first, because I think there's a griddle that's calling our names."

I knew the tradition, so I had to smile.

"Welcome-back pancakes!" we said at the same time. Mom's blueberry pancakes were my welcome-home-from-camp tradition. She always put ice cream on them to make them into smiley faces and wrote "XO" in syrup on my plate. I could already taste them. I stood up and followed Mom downstairs. Maybe she was right about things. This day was already getting a little bit better.

The next couple of days were a blur. On our last night in the house, we sat on the grass in the backyard. We had been packing and hauling boxes, and we were all sweaty and dirty and tired. Mom and Dad had emptied out the refrigerator and cabinets, so we had kind of a mishmash to eat. Tanner was eating cereal, peanut butter, crackers, and a hot dog that Dad had made on the grill. For dessert Mom pulled out the last carton of ice cream from the freezer, and since we had packed the bowls up, we all stuck spoons in and shared. "Hey!" I yelped as Tanner's spoon jabbed mine.

"I want those chocolate chips!" he said, digging in. Mom laughed. "In about a week we're going to have so much ice cream, we won't even know what to do with it!" Mom's store was opening soon, and since she was so busy with all the details, the packing at home hadn't exactly gone smoothly. Since Mom kept having to go to the store for things like the freezer delivery or to meet with people about things like what kind of spoons to order, we actually got Dad's apartment set up first. It was nice, but it was . . . well, weird. Tanner and I each had our own rooms, but they were kind of small. And Dad's house felt like Dad's, not really like our house. Dad had always loved modern things, so everything was glass and leather. It looked like it should be in a catalog. I was kind of afraid to mess anything up. There were a lot of pictures of me and of Tanner, but the first thing I noticed was that there were no pictures of the four of us.

"Where's the one from New Year's?" I asked, standing in front of a bookcase. We always took a family picture on New Year's Day.

Dad looked around. "Oh," he said, a little flustered. "I guess Mom took those shots. She has more room in the house."

I looked at him. *So this is how it's going to be,* I thought. *The three of us here and the three of us there.*

"We can take some new shots!" Dad said.

"Better," I kept whispering to myself. They'd both promised it was going to be better. But it wasn't really better. It was just downright weird.

The night before moving day, Tanner and I went to bed late. We had been packing all day, and we were beat, but I still couldn't sleep. I heard the back door open. I looked out my window and saw a shadow on the lawn. I almost freaked out, but then I realized that it was Mom, sitting on one of the rocking chairs that we'd bought for the new house but that had accidentally gotten delivered here. She was facing the house, and she looked like she was trying to memorize exactly the way it looked right then. I wondered if she could see me looking out at her. Then I saw Dad walk toward her. It was kind of weird that he was still here, since he had his apartment already, but they had decided that we would all move at the same time. Dad sat down on the grass next to Mom, and I could see them talking but couldn't hear what they were saying. I heard Mom laugh, and then I heard Dad laughing too. It was a nice sound. It was the last night we'd all be sleeping in this house together. I knew we were still a family—they kept telling us that—but it was the last time we'd all live together, and tomorrow morning everything was going to really change. I looked at

Mom and Dad laughing, but all it did was make my throat thick. Some things were too sad to see, so I flung myself into bed, hoping I'd fall asleep fast.

When the movers rolled up to the house early the next morning, Mom and Dad had already been up for hours, cleaning and sweeping and taking care of a lot of last-minute stuff. The house already didn't look like ours anymore.

When everything was loaded up, Mom locked the front door and handed Dad the key. We all stood there on the porch for a minute, looking up at the house. *Home.* I started to cry, and so did Mom. I buried my head in Dad's chest, and I could tell he was crying too. Only Tanner, who was sitting on the step playing a game on Dad's phone, seemed unmoved. "Tanner!" I yelled. "Say good-bye to your house!"

Tanner looked up, confused. "Uh, bye, house," he said, and we all laughed.

"Okay, troops," Mom said. "Onward." Tanner and I got into Mom's car, and we pulled out of the driveway. I looked back down our street as long as I could, saying good-bye to everything as it was.

We turned onto the main road, and Mom took a

deep breath. "Okay, gang," she said. "On to our next adventure! Here we go."

"To where?" Tanner asked.

"To our new house," Mom said, turning around to look at Tanner. "And to better things ahead."

"Oh," said Tanner. "I thought maybe we were going someplace fun." Mom looked at Tanner like he had ten heads. Then she looked at me, and we both cracked up. Some things, it seemed, weren't going to change at all.

Still Hungry?

There's always room for another Cupcake!

Coco Simon always dreamed of opening a cupcake bakery but was afraid she would eat all of the profits. When she's not daydreaming about cupcakes, Coco edits children's books and has written close to one hundred books for children, tweens, and young adults, which is a lot less than the number of cupcakes she's eaten. Cupcake Diaries is the first time Coco has mixed her love of cupcakes with writing.

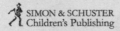

READ & LEARN
with *simon* kids

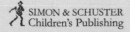

If you like **CUPCAKEDIARIES** books,
then you'll love

Also written by Coco Simon, they are another sweet treat!